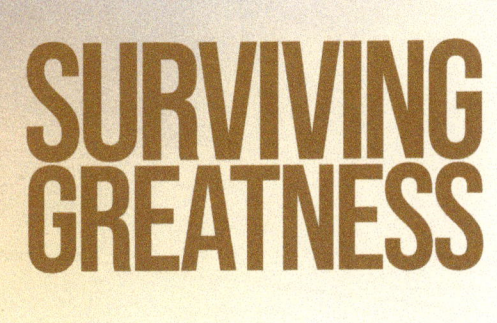

SURVIVING GREATNESS

Copyright ©2024 Jaime Taets

All rights reserved. No part of this publication may be reproduced, distributed or transmitted in any form or by any means, including photocopying, recording or other electronic methods, without prior written permission from the publisher, except in the case of brief quotations embodied in critical reviews and certain other noncommercial uses permitted by copyright law.

For permission requests, bulk purchase discounts, or U.S. trade bookstore and wholesaler orders, contact the publisher at **Info@JaimeTaets.com**

Cover Design, Interior Layout, and Creative by KrisVanderVies
KMDezine Studio, California

Artwork by Colleen Runné

Manufactured and printed in the United States of America, distributed globally by **Edgar Taets Publishing**.

HARDCOVER
ISBN: **978-1-965737-16-3**

AUDIO BOOK
ISBN: 978-1-965737-15-6

EBOOK
ISBN: 978-1-965737-14-9

SURVIVING GREATNESS

THE UNNERVING REALITY OF BEING BORN GREAT

JAIME TAETS

INSPIRED BY TRUE EVENTS

1 The Climbing Convention

• ● ● •

Nat stepped into the cavernous convention center, her senses immediately assaulted by a kaleidoscope of colors, sounds, and movement. Vibrant banners hung from the rafters, touting the latest in climbing gear and adventure destinations. The dull roar of hundreds of animated conversations echoed off the walls. Climbers of all ages and nationalities milled about, some clad in performance apparel from their sponsors, others sporting well-worn gear that had seen its share of cliffs and crags.

She took a deep breath, inhaling the distinct blend of new nylon, polished metal, and human exertion that defined these gatherings. Despite having attended countless conventions over the years, she still felt a thrill course through her veins, an electric current of shared passion and purpose.

Nat navigated through the throngs of attendees, her keen eyes scanning the array of booths and exhibits. She paused at a display of sleek new carabiners, their anodized finishes glinting under the bright lights.

The rep, a wiry twenty-something with an earnest grin, leaped into his pitch. "Natalia Rivera, as I live and breathe! You're just the person who needs to see this. We've shaved a full two ounces off the weight without compromising a bit of strength. Imagine what that could do for your speed on a multi-pitch route!"

Nat smiled politely, running a finger along the contoured edge of a carabiner. "Impressive. Though it's hard to beat tried-and-true methods."

The rep nodded vigorously, undeterred. "Of course, of course. But innovation, that's the key, right? You don't get to be the best without embracing progress."

Before Nat could respond, a voice called out from behind her. "Nat! Over here!"

She turned to see a cluster of fans, their faces alight with excitement.

A young girl, no more than twelve, held out a glossy poster emblazoned with Nat's image—a candid shot of her mid-climb, muscles coiled in concentration. "Could you sign this for me? You're my hero. I want to climb just like you someday."

"And climb you will," Nat said, taking the offered marker. She remembered being that girl, staring up at posters of her own idols, dreaming of summits yet unseen. She crouched down to the girl's level. "What's your name, sweetheart?"

"Jenna," the girl replied.

Nat scrawled a message on the poster. "To Jenna," she read aloud as she wrote. "Dream big, climb high, and never let anyone tell you it can't be done. Your friend, Nat."

She handed the poster back to the beaming girl, then spent the next several minutes signing autographs, posing for photos, and receiving the heartfelt thanks of her fans. It was a role she'd grown accustomed to, but one that never ceased to humble her.

As the last fan drifted away, Nat felt a hand clap her on the shoulder. She turned to find Tony Gallo, a fellow climber and longtime friendly rival.

"Nat, you're crushing it, as always!" Tony said with a grin. "Congrats on ascending that new route on Mount Fairweather. Heard it was a real nail-biter."

"Thanks, Tony," Nat said, returning his smile. "It was a fun challenge. It kept me on my toes."

Tony's smile melted. "But hey, what's this I hear about you turning down the keynote at the Apex Climbing Institute event next month? Thought for sure you'd be all over that."

Nat shrugged, trying to keep her tone nonchalant. "Just needed a break from the spotlight, you know? Wanted to focus on the climbing, not the talking."

Tony studied her for a moment, his brow furrowed. "Sure, sure. It's just not like you, is all. You've always been so gung ho about inspiring the next generation, paying it forward and all that."

Nat felt a twinge of defensiveness. If she was being honest with herself, she wasn't entirely sure why she'd declined the speaking gig. She'd told herself it was a scheduling conflict, that she needed to reserve her energy for training. But deep down, she knew there was more to it.

"Well, you know how it is," she said breezily. "Gotta mix things up every now and then."

Tony looked unconvinced, but he let the subject drop. They chatted a bit longer, swapping tales of recent climbs and future plans, before Tony excused himself to go check out a demo on ice-climbing techniques.

Left alone with her thoughts, Nat wandered through the convention hall. She paused here and there to examine a piece of gear or watch a clip of a daring ascent. Yet even as she went through the motions, her mind was elsewhere.

She thought about all the sacrifices she'd made to get to where she was. The birthdays and holidays missed, the relationships strained by her constant absence. The toll it had taken on her body, the scars and aches that had never quite faded. She'd always told herself it was worth it, that the accolades and the adrenaline rush of the summit made up for everything else.

But that calculation didn't add up the way it used to. The shine of each new achievement wore off faster than the last. The questions from well-meaning strangers—"What's next for you, Nat?" "How will you top that last climb, Nat?"—felt less like flattery and more like pressure.

"Miss Rivera!" a man called out from a nearby booth. He thrust out his hand. "Mark Johnson with Peak Performance. We're all big fans of yours."

Nat shook his hand warily, bracing herself for the inevitable pitch.

"You're exactly the kind of athlete we're looking to partner with," Mark continued, his smile wide and sharklike. "A real trailblazer, pun fully intended. We'd love to talk about a potential sponsorship deal, get you kitted out in our latest and greatest."

Nat had heard this spiel a hundred times from a hundred different companies. They all wanted a piece of her, a chance to cash in on her hard-won success. "I appreciate the offer, Mark, but I'm pretty happy with my current gear. And to be honest, I'm trying to step back from the whole sponsorship scene for a bit. Focus on the climbing itself, you know?"

Mark's smile didn't falter, but Nat could see a flicker of frustration in his eyes. "Sure, of course. But you know, strike while the iron is hot and all that. You're at the top of your game, Nat. Now's the time to capitalize on that, build your brand. Think of your legacy!"

Legacy. The word hit Nat like a punch to the gut. Is that what this was all about? Securing her place in the annals of climbing history? Leaving a mark that would endure long after her body had crumbled to dust?

She mumbled some polite but noncommittal response, then made her escape, pretending to spot someone she knew across the hall. She wove her way through the crowd, not sure where she was going, but feeling a desperate need to be anywhere but there.

As she walked, snippets of conversation drifted to her ears. A group of climbers debating the ethics of drilling bolts on remote peaks. A woman bemoaning the lack of diversity in the upper echelons of the sport. A teenager excitedly recounting the details of his first multi-pitch climb, involving multiple routes between belay points—the anchored points used to secure roped climbers to protect them from falling.

Nat paused, struck by a sudden thought. When was the last time she'd felt that kind of passion for climbing? Not the thrill of nailing a challenging move or standing atop a summit, but the deep, soul-level love for the act itself? The simple joy of solving the puzzle of the rock, of pushing her body and mind to their limits?

Somewhere along the way, that feeling had gotten buried under layers of expectation and obligation. Sponsorship requirements and media appearances and the constant pressure to one-up herself. She'd become so focused on the destination that she'd lost sight of the journey.

Shaking her head as if to clear it, she spotted a large crowd gathered before a small stage at the far end of the hall. A banner hung above it, emblazoned with the logo of a popular climbing magazine. As she watched, a woman in a bright green polo shirt stepped up to the microphone.

"Ladies and gentlemen," the woman announced, her voice booming over the PA system. "We have some of the biggest names in climbing under this very roof today, and who did we spot in the crowd just now? Winner of multiple World Cup

titles, first ascensionist of some of the most challenging routes on the planet, and all-around badass, please put your hands together for... Natalia Rivera!"

A spotlight swung toward Nat, catching her in its glare. She blinked, disoriented, as applause broke out around her.

"Come say hi to the fans, Nat!" The woman on stage beckoned, a too-bright smile plastered on her face.

Nat hesitated, resenting the ambush. In deference to the crowd, she played along, a fixed grin of her own emerging as she walked toward the stage. Climbing the small set of steps to the platform, she shook the woman's hand and turned to face the audience. A sea of expectant faces stared back at her, smartphones and cameras held aloft.

The interviewer, whose name tag identified her as Lisa, launched into her questions without preamble. "Nat, you've had an incredible few years. Multiple first ascents, breaking speed records left and right. How do you stay motivated to keep pushing yourself to new heights?"

Nat paused, the practiced response she'd given dozens of times before hovering on the tip of her tongue. Something about training hard, staying focused, always seeking out new challenges. But the words felt hollow, rote. "You know, Lisa, I think sometimes we get so caught up in chasing the next big thing that we lose sight of why we started climbing in the first place. For the love of it, you know? The pure, simple joy of moving over stone."

Taken aback by the response, Lisa recovered quickly. "So, are you saying you're thinking of taking a step back? Slowing down a bit?"

Nat shook her head. "No, not exactly. I still love climbing, still want to push myself. But I'm realizing that maybe I need to recalibrate a bit. Focus less on the external goals and more on the internal experience. Really tune in to what lights me up."

"And what does light you up these days?" Lisa asked, leaning forward with a conspiratorial air.

Nat thought for a moment. What still sparked that flame inside her, that deep sense of purpose and passion? "Mentorship, for one. Working with young climbers, sharing what I've learned. Helping them to not just climb hard, but to approach the sport—and life—with intention and integrity." She paused.

"And on a personal level, I want to strip it back to the essentials. Choose objectives not because they'll look good on Instagram, but because they scare me a little. Because they'll require me to grow, as a climber and as a person."

"Growth is certainly a major theme of your career," Lisa said. "You've never been one to rest on your laurels. So what's next for you? What new challenges are on the horizon?"

Nat hesitated, the question hitting a nerve. It was the same one she'd been asking herself for months—the one she'd avoided every time it came up in interviews or casual conversation.

"Honestly, Lisa?" she said, deciding to throw caution to the wind. "I don't know. And for the first time in a long time, I'm okay with that. I think sometimes, not knowing is a good thing. It means you're open to possibilities, to letting the path reveal itself as you go."

She could feel the surprise rippling through the crowd, could see it reflected in Lisa's arched eyebrows. Natalia Rivera, always so certain, so focused, admitting to uncertainty? It was unheard of. But Nat felt a strange sense of lightness as the words left her mouth. As if a weight she'd been carrying for years had suddenly lifted from her shoulders.

The interview wrapped up quickly after that. Lisa thanked her for her time and insight. Nat stepped down from the stage in a daze, adrenaline still thrumming through her veins. She was just about to make a beeline for the exit, desperate for some fresh air and solitude, when a voice from the crowd stopped her in her tracks.

"Nat! Hey, Nat!"

She turned to see Bryan, a fellow climber and occasional training partner, pushing his way toward her.

"Hey, thanks for the book recommendation," he said, placing a hardcover book in her hands. "Finally got around to reading it. Oh, and great interview, by the way. I dig what you're saying."

"Hey, Bryan. Thanks." Nat turned the book over, running an affectionate hand over the cover—*Vertical Wisdom* by Evelyn Blackwell. "Glad you liked the book. I think I'm due for a reread."

"Well, guess what?" Bryan said. "She's here! Doing a signing at the Adventure Books booth. Figured you might want to check it out, maybe get your copy signed."

SURVIVING GREATNESS

"Really? Right now?" Nat felt a jolt of excitement as Bryan nodded. Evelyn Blackwell was a personal hero of hers—a living legend, one of the pioneers of modern rock climbing. Nat had devoured her memoir, marveling at the way Evelyn wove together tales of her epic ascents with profound insights about life, loss, and the human condition. Nat had a feeling it was this book that had spurned many of the questions she'd been dealing with lately.

The chance to meet her hero in person was too good to pass up. Nat thanked Bryan for the tip and set off in search of the Adventure Books booth.

The Climbing Convention

2 Meeting Evelyn Blackwell

• • • •

Nat navigated through the bustling convention hall, her eyes scanning the myriad of booths for the Adventure Books display. The excited chatter of attendees and the occasional bursts of laughter created a lively ambiance, but her focus was solely on locating Evelyn Blackwell.

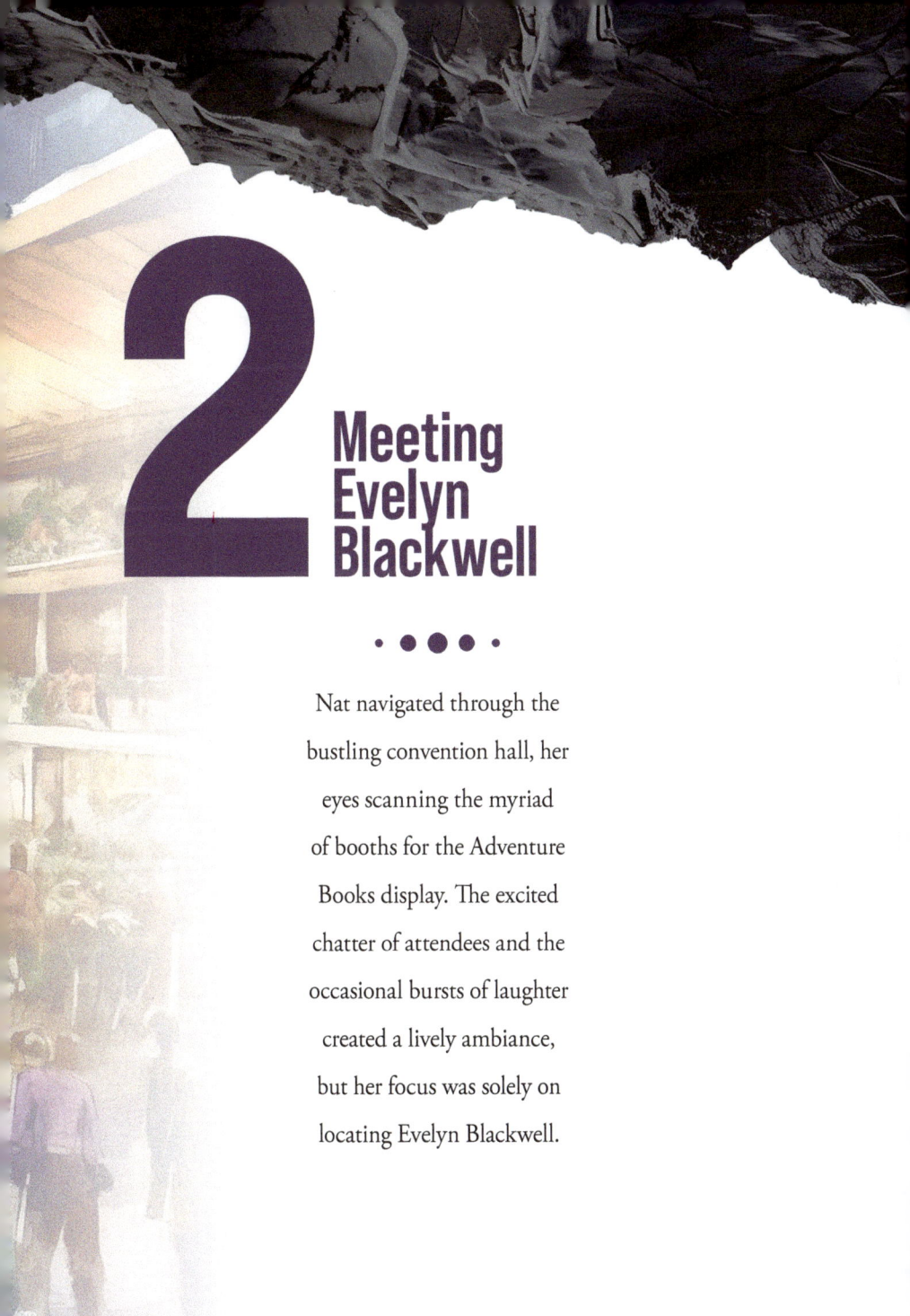

After a few minutes of weaving through the crowd, Nat finally spotted the booth. A large banner featuring Evelyn's book cover hung above it, announcing her presence. Nat's heart raced as she approached, taking in the sight of her climbing hero talking with the next fan in line.

A slender woman in her sixties, with short silver hair and piercing blue eyes, Evelyn radiated an aura of calm confidence. She greeted each person with a warm smile and a firm handshake, her attention fully focused on the individual before her. Nat watched as Evelyn listened intently to a young woman sharing her own climbing experiences, nodding encouragingly and offering words of support.

Nat joined the line, her nervousness growing with each step closer to the table. Nearly half an hour later, she was next in line. The man ahead of her gushed to Evelyn about how her book had inspired him to take up climbing in his forties, despite his fear of heights. Evelyn listened attentively, her eyes shining with genuine delight at his story.

"That's wonderful!" she said, clasping the man's hand between her own. "It's never too late to face our fears and discover new passions. Keep climbing, my friend, and remember—the most rewarding views come after the hardest ascents."

The man thanked her profusely, his face beaming as he stepped away from the table. Nat marveled at Evelyn's ability to connect with her fans on such a deep level, to offer wisdom and encouragement so effortlessly.

Evelyn looked up as Nat approached the table, a flicker of recognition crossing her face, followed by a warm smile. "Natalia Rivera! This is a real pleasure. I've been following your career with great admiration."

Nat felt her cheeks flush as she shook Evelyn's hand. "Thank you, Evelyn. That means a great deal coming from you. Your book, your climbs… you've been such an inspiration to me."

"We draw inspiration from each other," Evelyn said, her gaze intense and searching. "In climbing and in life." Taking Nat's book, she opened the cover and paused for a moment, pen poised above the title page. Then, with a few swift strokes, she handed it back.

Nat glanced down at the inscription, her breath catching at the words Evelyn had chosen: *To Natalia—May your journey always lead you higher, on and off the rock. Evelyn Blackwell.* Nat looked back up to find Evelyn studying her intently, a knowing glint in her eye.

"You know," Evelyn said, "I sense there's more on your mind than just an autograph. I've been in this game a long time. I can tell when someone is grappling with big questions."

Nat felt a jolt of surprise at Evelyn's observation. She hesitated, glancing back at the line of fans still waiting their turn.

Evelyn followed her gaze and smiled. "Tell you what," she said, reaching for a scrap of paper and scribbling something on it. "I'll be here for another hour or so. Why don't you come find me after, and we can chat more privately? I have a feeling you and I might have a lot to talk about."

She handed Nat the paper, which bore a hastily sketched map of the convention center with an X marking a spot in the food court.

A mix of excitement and trepidation swirled in Nat's gut. "I... yes, thank you. I'd like that very much."

Evelyn nodded, her smile warm and conspiratorial. "Until then, Natalia. Enjoy the rest of the convention. And

remember, keep your eyes open. Wisdom can be found in unexpected places."

With that cryptic piece of advice, Nat walked away from the booth in a daze, clutching the signed book and the map to her chest. She wandered the convention floor in a daze, her mind buzzing with anticipation. She stopped at a few booths that caught her eye—a display of eco-friendly climbing ropes, a virtual reality simulation of a famous route in Yosemite—but found it hard to focus.

Instead, her thoughts kept drifting back to Evelyn's inscription in her book. *May your journey always lead you higher, on and off the rock.* It was such a simple sentiment, yet it resonated deeply with Nat. Wasn't that what she'd been searching for all along? A journey that went beyond just the physical act of climbing, that challenged her to grow and evolve as a person?

She thought back to her own climbing career, the highs and lows she'd experienced over the years. The euphoria of topping out on a long-sought-after route, the crushing disappointment of falling just short of a goal. The camaraderie of the climbing community, the solitude of a solo ascent. Why did it feel like that wasn't enough anymore?

Suddenly, a familiar voice called out from behind her. "Nat? Natalia Rivera, is that you?"

Nat turned to find herself face to face with an old climbing buddy, Sarah, whom she hadn't seen in years.

Sarah's face lit up as she pulled Nat into a warm embrace. "Oh my gosh, Nat! It's been so long!" She stepped back to get a better look at her friend. "You look amazing! Your career has been unreal. I'm just so thrilled for you!"

"Sarah?" Nat said. "Wow, it's great to see you! What have you been up to?"

Sarah laughed, shaking her head. "Oh, you know, still climbing whenever I can. But I decided to focus on my career instead of going pro. Enough about me, though. I want to hear about you! What are you working on? Any big climbs coming up?"

Nat's smile faltered, and she shrugged. "Honestly, I'm just trying to figure that out."

"Well, you've got all the options in the world, so no wonder you're having a hard time deciding!"

"Yeah," Nat said with a chuckle. That wasn't exactly the problem, but she didn't see the point in correcting her.

A group of Sarah's friends called out to her as they rushed by. "I'm so sorry, Nat. I have to run. We're late to a panel discussion. But it was so great to see you! Let's keep in touch. I'll find you on socials!"

With a final hug, Sarah disappeared into the crowd. As Nat continued wandering the hall, she reflected on her strange predicament. The earlier lightness she'd felt when admitting she didn't know what was next had disappeared. She'd told Lisa and the crowd that she was okay with it, but running into Sarah made her realize that wasn't the case. Far from it, in fact. She didn't mind not knowing what was next—provided she knew *why* she didn't know. And the simple fact was, she didn't have a clue.

Success, it seemed, was a double-edged sword. She had burst onto the climbing scene years ago with her audacious ascent of the Emperor Face on Canada's Mount Robson, a sheer 2,500-foot wall of ice and rock that had never been climbed in a single push. The climbing world had watched

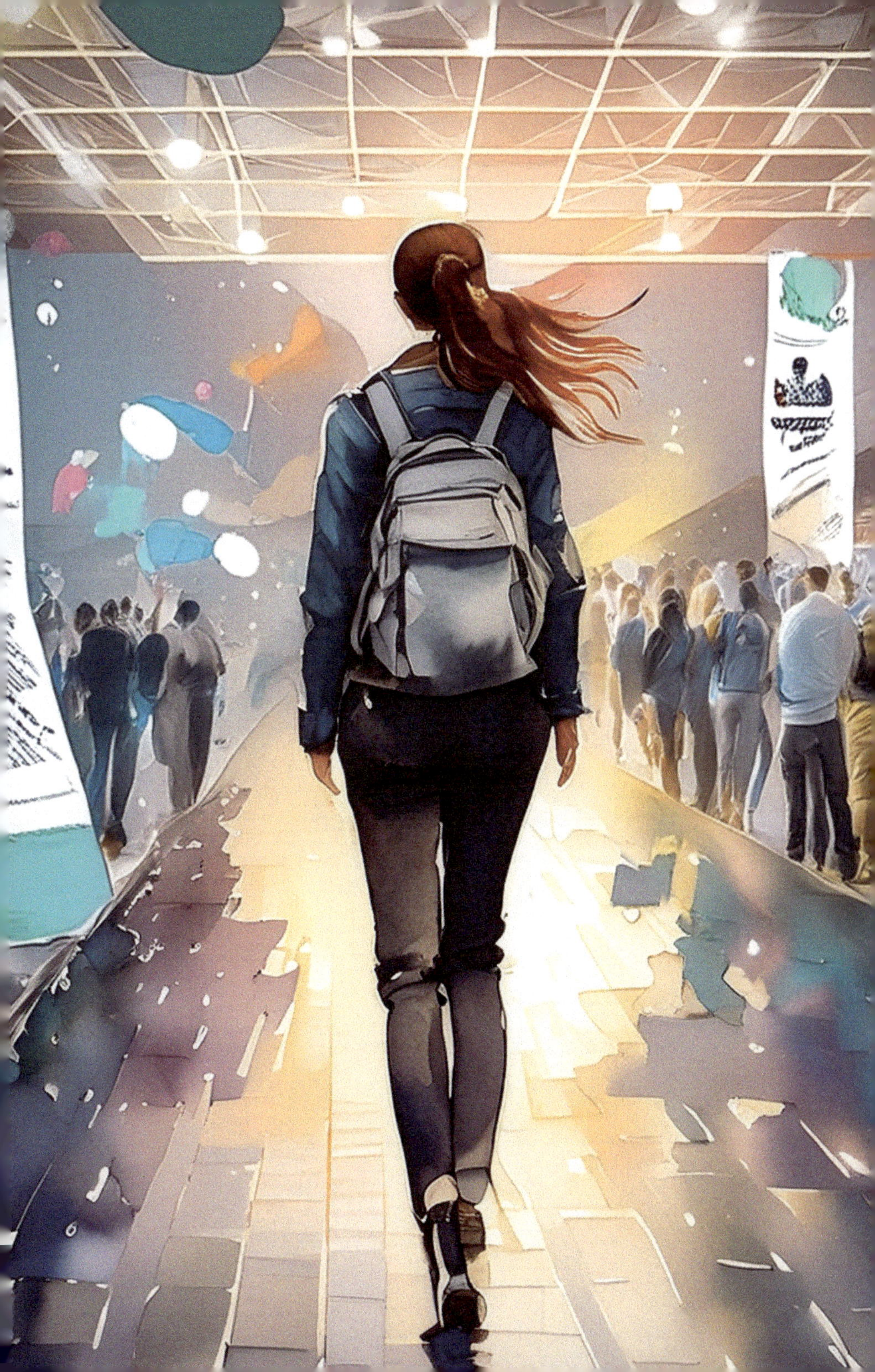

in awe as she battled up the unforgiving face, her movements fluid and relentless, etching her name into the annals of mountaineering history.

From there, she had established groundbreaking routes on some of the world's most challenging peaks. In the Andes, she had pioneered the first ascent of the South Face of Aconcagua, a sweeping wall of bullet-hard ice and crumbling rock that had repelled countless elite alpinists. And in Patagonia, she had made a daring solo ascent of Cerro Torre's infamous Southeast Ridge, battling mile-a-minute winds and treacherous rime ice to tag the summit of one of the most daunting spires in the Southern Hemisphere.

These feats and a dozen others had brought her fame, recognition, and the opportunity to inspire others. Yet it all left her feeling lost and unprepared for whatever was next. She had never imagined that standing at the peak of her climbing career would leave her feeling so adrift.

A thought occurred to her, freezing her where she stood. *Success is supposed to be a destination, isn't it?* Or was success the obstacle keeping her from finding her true purpose?

Her watch buzzed at her wrist, rescuing her from a rabbit hole of despair. It was nearly time for her meeting with Evelyn.

Shoving the epiphany aside, she consulted the map, orienting herself in the sprawling convention center. The food court was on the opposite end of the building, past the main stage where the morning's keynote speech had taken place. Nat set off at a brisk pace, weaving through the throngs of attendees with a new sense of purpose. She couldn't explain it, but she felt like she was on the cusp of something big, some revelation that had been eluding her for years.

As she walked, snippets of conversations drifted past her. Mostly, climbers debated the finer points of technique and gear. Others swapped beta stories, recounting how they had decided on the route they would take before tackling a climb. But for once, Nat found herself tuning out the chatter, her focus turned inward. She thought of Evelyn's cryptic parting words—*Wisdom can be found in unexpected places.* Was this what she meant? That the answers Nat sought might not be found at the summit or on the winner's podium, but in the quiet moments and chance encounters of everyday life?

Once at the food court, she scanned the sea of tables for a familiar silver-haired figure, finding her at a small table tucked away in a corner. Evelyn was alone, sipping from a steaming mug as she jotted notes in a small leather-bound journal.

Evelyn looked up as Nat approached, her face breaking into a warm smile. "Glad you could make it. Have a seat."

Meeting Evelyn Blackwell

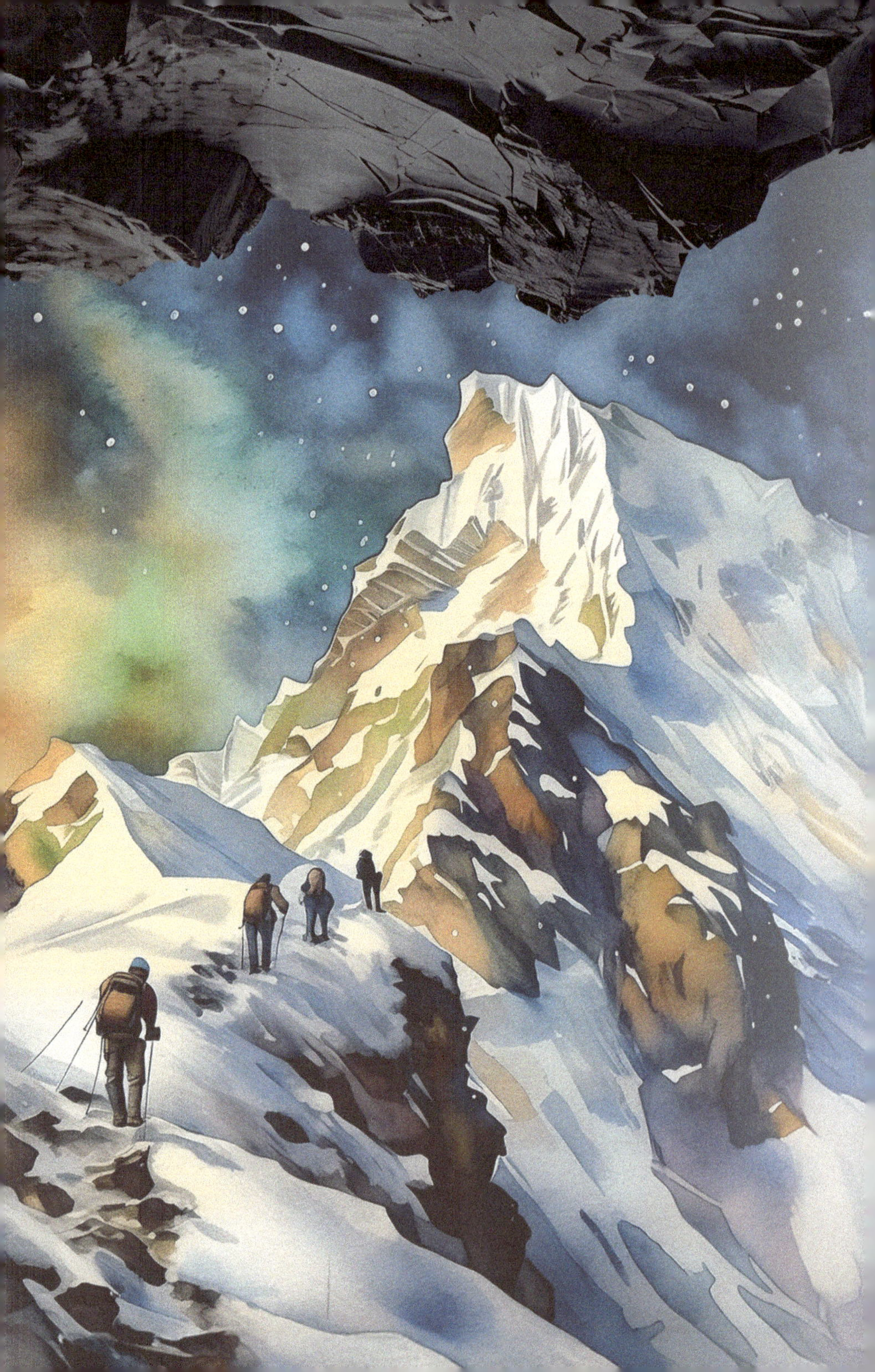

3
A Journey Begins

• • • •

Nat slid into the chair across from Evelyn, her heart pounding with a mixture of nerves and excitement. Up close, Evelyn's presence was even more commanding, her blue eyes sharp and penetrating.

"I have to admit," Nat said, fiddling with the sleeve of her hoodie, "I'm not entirely sure where to start. I have so many questions, so many things I want to ask you."

Evelyn chuckled, a rich sound that seemed to come from the very center of her being. "The hardest part is always starting," she said, echoing the opening line of her book. "But once we take that first step, the path begins to reveal itself." She leaned forward, fixing Nat with an intense gaze. "So tell me, Natalia. What brings you to this moment? What's weighing on your heart?"

Nat took a deep breath, feeling the weight of Evelyn's undivided attention. She thought of all the challenges and triumphs that had led her to this point, all the questions and doubts that had been building inside her for months—years, even.

And with a sudden clarity, she knew exactly where to begin. "I guess I'm wondering what it all means. The climbing, the competing, the constant push to be better, faster, stronger. I've achieved so much in my career, but lately it feels like there's something missing. Like I'm chasing after something I can't quite name."

"Ah," Evelyn said. "The eternal question. The search for meaning, for purpose. It's a journey we all must take, sooner or later." She took a sip of her tea, gathering her thoughts. "You know, I've been climbing for over fifty years. I've seen the sport change in ways I never could have imagined, seen generations of climbers come and go. And in all that time, do you know what I've learned?"

"What?" Nat said.

"That the summit is never the end goal," Evelyn replied. "It's the journey that matters, the lessons we learn along the way. The people we meet, the experiences we have, the ways in which we are tested and transformed. Climbing is a metaphor, Natalia. For life, for growth, for the human experience. We're all climbing our own mountains, facing our own challenges and fears. It's not about reaching the top. Not really. It's about who we become in the process."

Nat chewed her lip for a moment. "I wonder, if I'd known that at the start, maybe I'd be in a better position to deal with where I'm at now. I thought things would get easier at the top, not harder."

"It's lonely at the top for a reason, kiddo. Of the few who reach it, most just turn around and climb back down, believing that's all there is. They fail to see that the top is where the real journey begins."

"But where?" Nat pressed. "You can't go any higher. Where else is there to go?"

Evelyn smiled. "Inward."

Nat just stared at her, trying to process this new perspective.

"Success is its own challenge," Evelyn continued. "The biggest and most important of your life. You and I both spent our early careers clinging to the sides of mountains, knowing beyond doubt that *this* was our purpose. But then, one day, we realized that all those climbs, all those summits, were merely *leading* us to our purpose. This is what you're grappling with now. This is where so many fail to look inward and instead turn back or stay stuck in the same place."

"How did you find it?" Nat asked. "The deeper meaning, the purpose?"

"It found me," Evelyn said simply. "In the form of some remarkably wise Sherpas, on some of the most challenging climbs of my life. They guided me not just up the mountain, but toward a whole new way of seeing the world. Each one imparted a profound lesson, a nugget of wisdom that shifted my perspective in ways I never could have imagined."

Nat was struck by the uncanny parallels between Evelyn's story and her own inner journey. "I wonder if they could help me the same way they helped you."

Evelyn paused, studying Nat. "I believe they can. I've been thinking about revisiting those climbs, those lessons. And I think you should join me."

Nat's heart leaped. "Really?"

"Why not?" Evelyn replied, a mischievous glint in her eye. "I have a sense that you're ready for this, Natalia. That you're standing on the cusp of a great discovery, a great awakening. I'd be honored to guide you, to share what I've learned and perhaps even learn a thing or two myself in the process."

"I don't know what to say," Nat said, grinning from ear to ear, "except yes. Absolutely yes. And thank you."

"It's my pleasure," Evelyn said, waving away her thanks. "I have a feeling this will be just as rewarding for me as it will be for you."

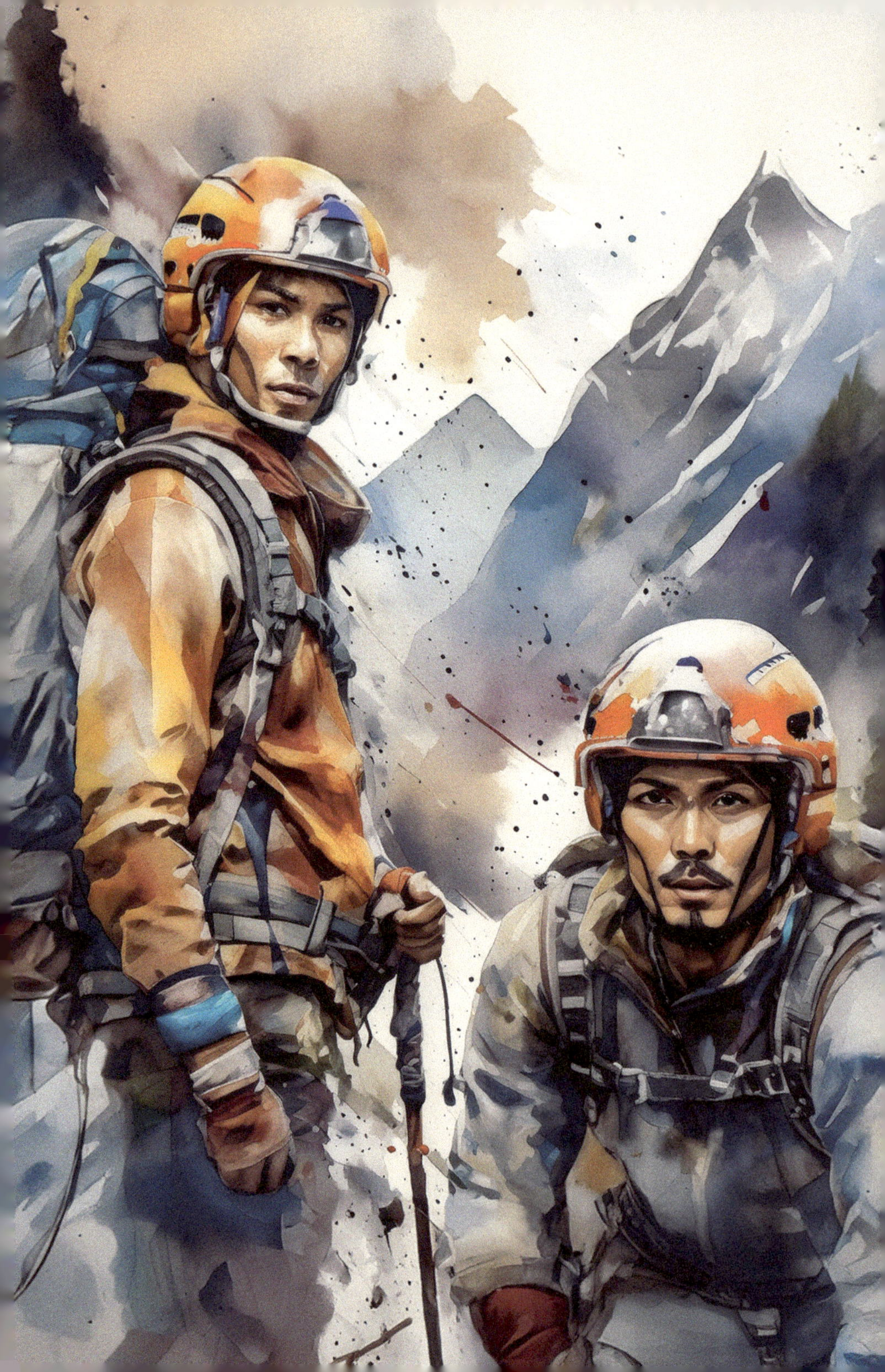

"Tell me more about the Sherpas," Nat said. "What specific lessons did they teach you?"

Evelyn smiled. "Tenzin, he was always reminding me to pause and appreciate the little things. 'Every step is a gift,' he'd say. 'Every breath, a blessing.' And Lhakpa, he pushed me beyond what I thought I was capable of. 'The mountain doesn't care about your limits,' he'd grunt as we climbed. 'Only you do.' And Tashi, oh, he could find humor in anything. 'Why so serious?' he'd tease when the going got tough. 'Smile, laugh, live. That's the secret to the summit.'"

"It sounds like they each had such unique perspectives."

"That's the beauty of it," Evelyn said. "Every climb, every Sherpa, every moment—they each have something to teach us, if we're open to it. That's where the real growth happens, when we allow ourselves to be challenged, to be cracked open and put back together in new and beautiful ways."

As the convention center began to empty out around them, Nat and Evelyn lingered at the table, ironing out the details of their impending adventure.

"So, I'm thinking we start with the Matterhorn," Evelyn said, tracing a finger over a map of the Swiss Alps. "I know a Sherpa there, Tenzin, who's a master at reading the mountain's moods."

"And then maybe Trango Tower in Pakistan?" Nat suggested. "I've always dreamed of climbing that one."

"Perfect," Evelyn said, jotting down notes. "Lhakpa knows those peaks like the back of his hand. He's a bit of a hard-ass, but he'll push us to be our best."

"I can't believe this is really happening," Nat said, shaking her head in wonder. "I feel like I'm about to embark on the adventure of a lifetime."

"You are," Evelyn said, reaching across the table to squeeze Nat's hand. "And I'm so glad I get to be a part of it. I have a feeling this is just the beginning of a beautiful friendship."

Nat squeezed back. "Me too."

They parted ways a while later with a promise to reconnect soon.

"I'll email you the flight details as soon as I have them," Evelyn said, shouldering her bag. "And Nat? Start training. We've got some big mountains to climb."

Nat grinned, already planning her workouts. "I'll be ready. See you soon. And thanks again for everything."

As Nat walked out of the convention center and into the fading light of evening, she felt a new fire in her heart. She didn't know exactly what the future held, but she knew enough. Her unformed questions had coalesced, been given shape. She had a direction now, with the promise of answers.

Even better, she had a guide to help her find them.

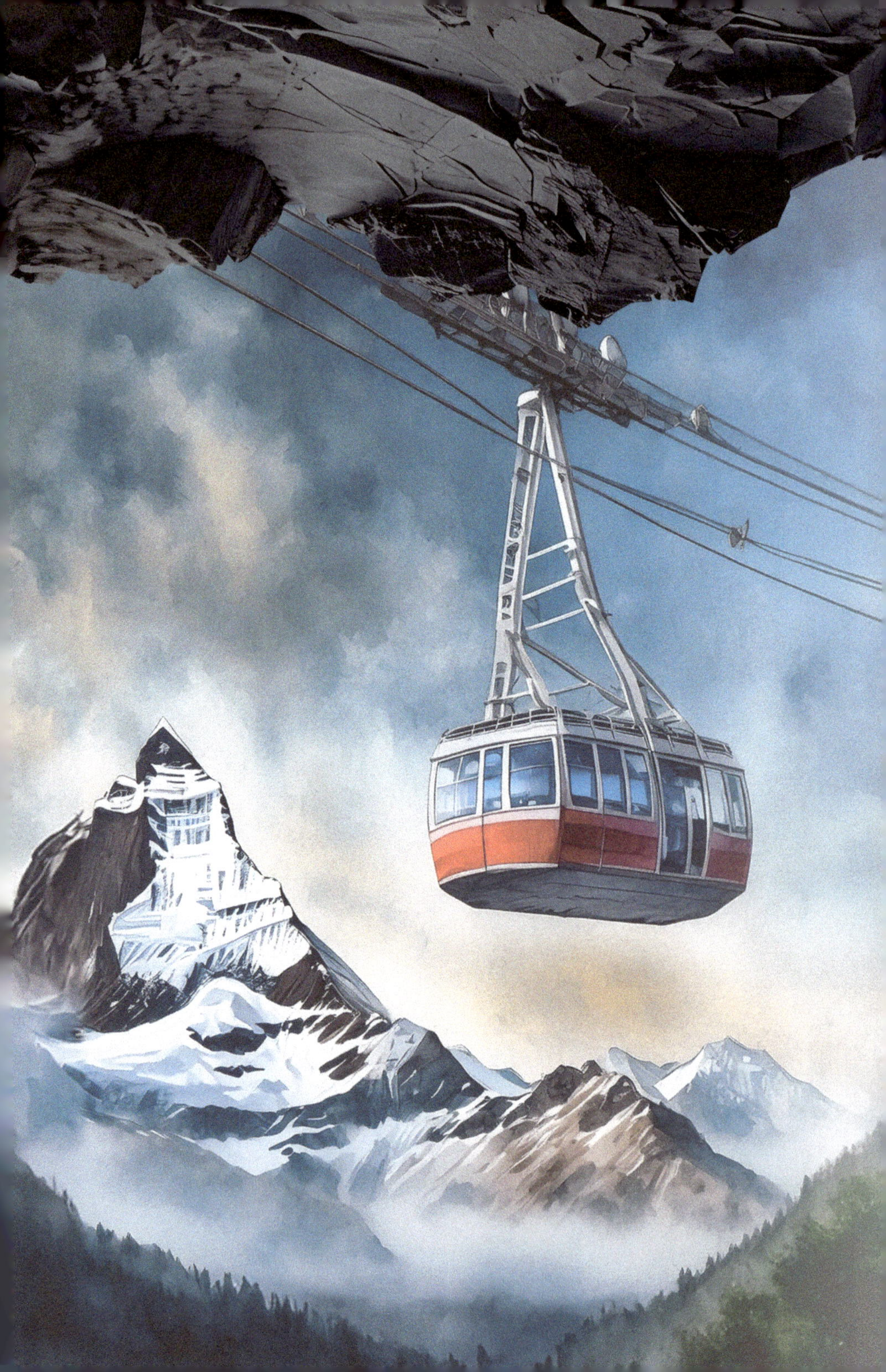

4 The Smallest Moments

• • • • •

Nat stepped out of the cable car and onto the snow-dusted platform, her breath catching at the sight before her. The Matterhorn loomed ahead, its iconic pyramidal peak piercing the crisp alpine sky. The early morning sun cast a rosy glow on the mountain's rugged face, highlighting the jagged ridges and deep crevasses that seemed to whisper of the challenges to come.

Beside her, Evie took a deep breath. "Never gets old, does it? No matter how many times I come here, that first glimpse of the mountain always takes my breath away."

Nat nodded, too awestruck to speak. She had climbed her fair share of iconic peaks, but there was something about the Matterhorn that felt different, almost reverent. It was as if the mountain was a living, breathing entity, a silent guardian watching over the valley below.

As they made their way toward the base of the climb, a figure emerged from a small cluster of buildings nearby. He was short and wiry, with weathered brown skin and a shock of black hair peeking out from under a well-worn hat. His face split into a wide grin as he spotted Evie, his eyes crinkling at the corners.

"Evie, my old friend!" he called out, striding toward them with open arms. "Welcome back to my mountain!"

Evie laughed, stepping forward to embrace the man. "Tenzin! I should have known you'd be here to greet us."

Tenzin chuckled. "Where else would I be? The Matterhorn and I, we have a special bond." He turned to Nat, appraising her with a keen gaze. "And you must be Natalia, the young climber I've heard so much about."

"Just Nat, please," she said, extending a hand. "It's an honor to meet you, Tenzin. Evie has told me so much about you and your wisdom of the mountain."

Tenzin grasped her hand, his grip strong and calloused. "Wisdom?" he scoffed, shaking his head. "I just listen to what the mountain tells me. She's the wise one, not me." He gestured for them to follow, leading them toward a small tent set up near the base of the route. "Come, let's have some tea before we start. The mountain will wait for us."

Inside the tent, Tenzin busied himself with a small stove, heating water and measuring out fragrant leaves into chipped enamel cups. As they waited for the tea to steep, he regaled them with tales of his recent climbs, his eyes gleaming with pleasure as he recounted narrow escapes and breathtaking summits.

Nat found herself drawn in by his infectious enthusiasm, his deep love for the mountains evident in every word. It was a passion she recognized, a fire that burned in her own veins.

As they sipped their tea, Tenzin turned to Nat, his expression growing serious. "So, young Nat. What brings you to my mountain? What do you seek here?"

Nat hesitated. "I'm not entirely sure. I guess I'm hoping to find some answers, some clarity on my path forward."

Tenzin nodded, as if he had expected this response. "Ah, yes. The search for meaning and purpose. It's a path we all must take, in our own time and in our own way." He held up a finger, his voice low and intense. "But let me tell you a secret, young Nat. The answers you seek? They're not up there." He pointed toward the peak of the Matterhorn, looming above them. "They're in here." He tapped a finger against his chest, over his heart. "And the only way to find them is to listen, to pay attention to the signs and whispers all around you."

Nat frowned, puzzled by his words. "Signs? Whispers? I'm not sure I understand."

Tenzin smiled, a mischievous glint in his eye. "You will, in time. The mountain will make sure of that." He drained the last of his tea and stood, stretching his arms overhead. "But enough talk. The day grows short, and we have a long climb ahead of us. Let's go and see what lessons the Matterhorn has in store for you today."

They set off up the mountain, the air growing thinner and colder with each step. Nat focused on her breathing, finding a steady rhythm as she navigated the rocky terrain. Ahead of her, Tenzin moved with the sure-footed grace of a mountain goat, his brightly colored jacket a beacon against the gray stone.

As they climbed higher, Nat found her mind wandering, drifting back to Tenzin's enigmatic words at the base. Signs and whispers, lessons waiting to be learned. What did he mean? How was she supposed to find answers in the unforgiving landscape of rock and ice? Lost in thought, she nearly missed Tenzin's shout from up ahead.

"Nat! Come and see this!"

She hurried to catch up, rounding a bend in the trail to find Tenzin and Evie crouched beside a small outcropping of rock. He was peering intently at something, a look of wonder on his face. There, clinging tenaciously to a tiny crack in the stone, was a small clump of flowers. Their delicate petals were a shocking blue against the dull gray of the rock, their slender stems trembling in the icy wind.

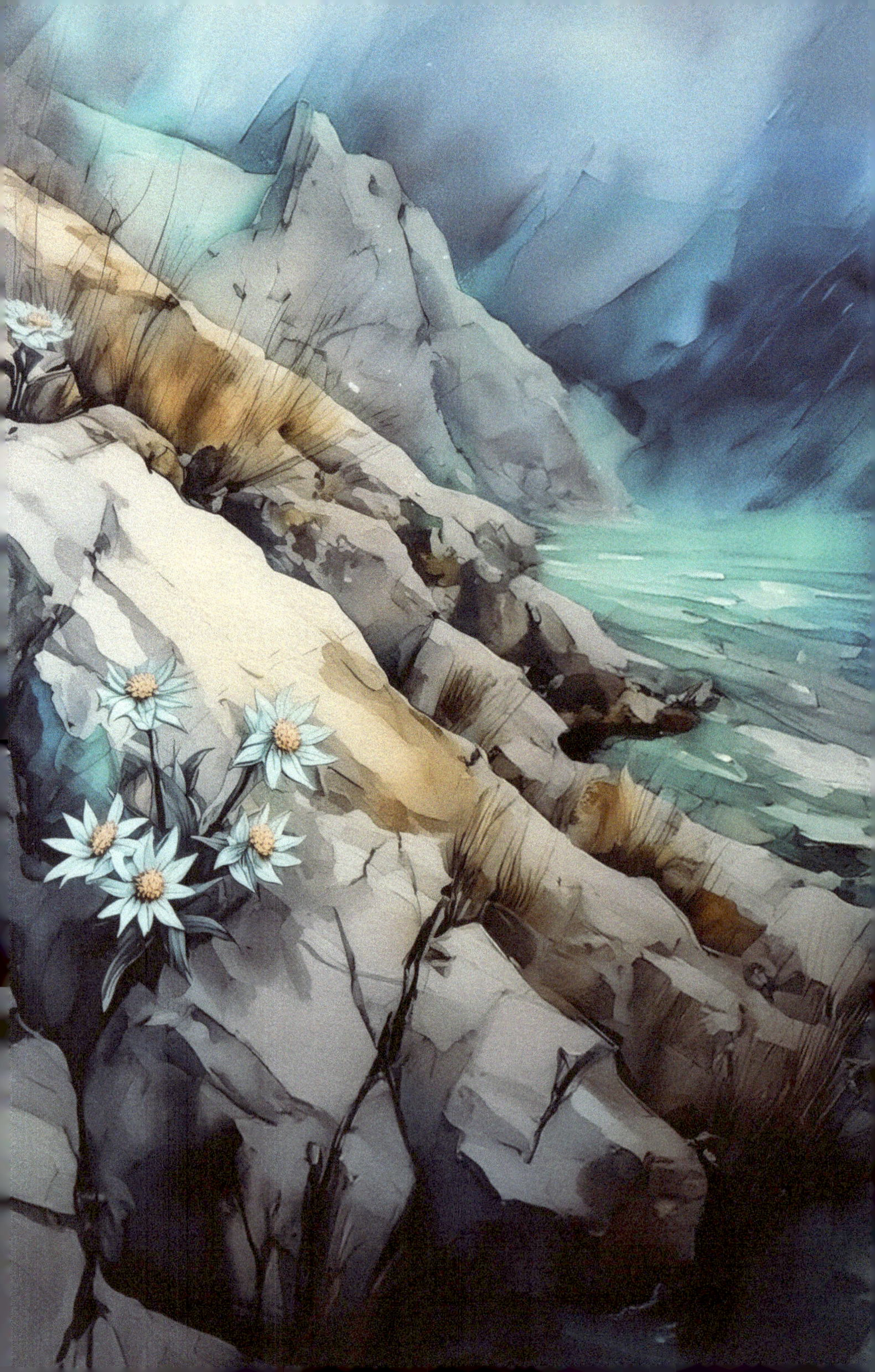

"Edelweiss," Tenzin said reverently, running a gentle finger over the velvety blooms. "The noble flower of the Alps. They grow only in the harshest of conditions, rooting themselves in places where nothing else dares to thrive. He looked up at Nat, his eyes shining with a fierce light. "There's a lesson here, young Nat. A message, if you're willing to hear it."

Nat kneeled beside him, studying the tiny flowers with newfound appreciation. "What do they tell you?"

"They tell me that success leaves clues," he said. "That even in the most challenging of circumstances, there is always a way forward. You just have to know where to look." He stood, brushing off his knees. "The mountain speaks to those who listen, Nat. It's up to us to pay attention, to be open to the wisdom it offers."

With that, they set off again, leaving Nat to ponder his words.

As they climbed higher, the air growing thinner and the terrain more treacherous, Nat scanned her surroundings with new eyes. She noticed the way the rocks fit together like puzzle pieces, creating a natural staircase up the mountain's face. She saw the delicate tracery of frost on the boulders, the glint of quartz catching the sun like a wink from the mountain itself.

And with each step, each breath, she felt a growing sense of connection, of understanding, as if the Matterhorn were whispering its secrets to her, guiding her toward some greater truth.

Ahead of her, Evie paused, turning to look back at Nat. "Feels different this time, doesn't it? I remember my first climb with Tenzin, how I was so focused on reaching the summit that I nearly missed all the beauty around me." She shook her head, laughing at the memory. "He had to practically yell at me to get me to stop and look, to really see the mountain for what it was. And when I did, it was like a revelation. Like I was seeing the world through new eyes."

Nat thought back to her own past climbs as she caught up to Evie. How many times had she been so laser-focused on the end goal, on ticking off another peak on her list, that she had failed to appreciate the journey itself? How many small moments of wonder and discovery had she missed in her single-minded pursuit of the summit? "I think I'm starting to understand. It's not just about getting to the top, is it? It's about being present, about learning from each step along the way."

Evie grinned, clapping Nat on the shoulder. "Exactly. The summit is just a bonus, a cherry on top of the sundae. The real reward is in the climb itself, in the challenges we face and the lessons we learn." She turned to look up at the peak, still so far above them. "Tenzin taught me that, all those years ago. And it's a lesson I've carried with me ever since, on every mountain and in every aspect of my life."

With renewed purpose, they continued their ascent, Tenzin setting a steady pace as they navigated the increasingly difficult terrain. Nat fell into a kind of meditative state, her mind clear and focused as she flowed over the rock and ice. And then, just as they were approaching a particularly challenging section of the climb, Tenzin called for a halt.

He pointed to a jagged outcropping of stone just ahead, his expression grave. "Do you see that, Nat? The way the rock is fractured, the loose rubble at the base?"

Nat peered at the spot, noting the spiderweb of cracks and the precarious pile of loose, rocky debris, commonly known as scree. "I see it. It looks unstable, dangerous."

Tenzin nodded, his eyes never leaving the rock face. "I've seen this before, on other climbs. It's a warning. A sign that the mountain is shifting, changing. To ignore it would be to invite disaster." He turned to face Nat, his expression intense. "There was a climber, years ago, who didn't heed this warning. He was young and brash, convinced of his own invincibility. He charged ahead, despite the mountain's message to turn back." Tenzin shook his head. "The rockfall was sudden, catastrophic. He was swept away in an instant, buried under tons of rubble. We never found his body."

Nat felt a chill run through her, a visceral reminder of the risks they faced on the mountain. "How do you know? How do you read the signs, hear the warnings?"

Tenzin smiled, the sadness in his eyes replaced by a fierce, burning wisdom. "By listening, Nat. By opening yourself to the mountain, letting it speak to you in its own language. The warnings are always there, the clues and whispers. We just have to be still enough, quiet enough, to hear them." He gestured to the crack in the rock, the loose scree. "This, here? This is the Matterhorn telling us to find another way, to respect its power and its boundaries. And if we're wise, we'll listen."

Nat nodded, a newfound sense of respect and humility washing over her. She realized, with a startling clarity, that this was what she had been missing all along. This deep, intuitive connection to the mountains she climbed, this willingness to let them guide her, teach her, shape her.

With Tenzin leading the way, they carefully skirted the unstable section of rock, finding a safer path up the face. As they climbed, Nat felt the shifts, the subtle whispers she had been too busy, too goal-oriented to hear before. In the way the wind sang through the crags, in the patterns of sunlight and shadow on the snow. In the small, hardy plants that clung to the crevices, the tiny paw prints of unseen creatures. The mountain was speaking to her. And for the first time, she was ready to listen.

They reached a small plateau, a natural resting point before the final push to the summit. As they paused to catch their breath and take in the sweeping vista below, Tenzin turned to Nat with a smile. "You feel it, don't you? The mountain's wisdom, its lessons?"

Nat nodded, too moved to speak.

Beside her, Evie grinned, her expression a mirror of Tenzin's own. "It's a special thing, to be attuned to the mountain like this."

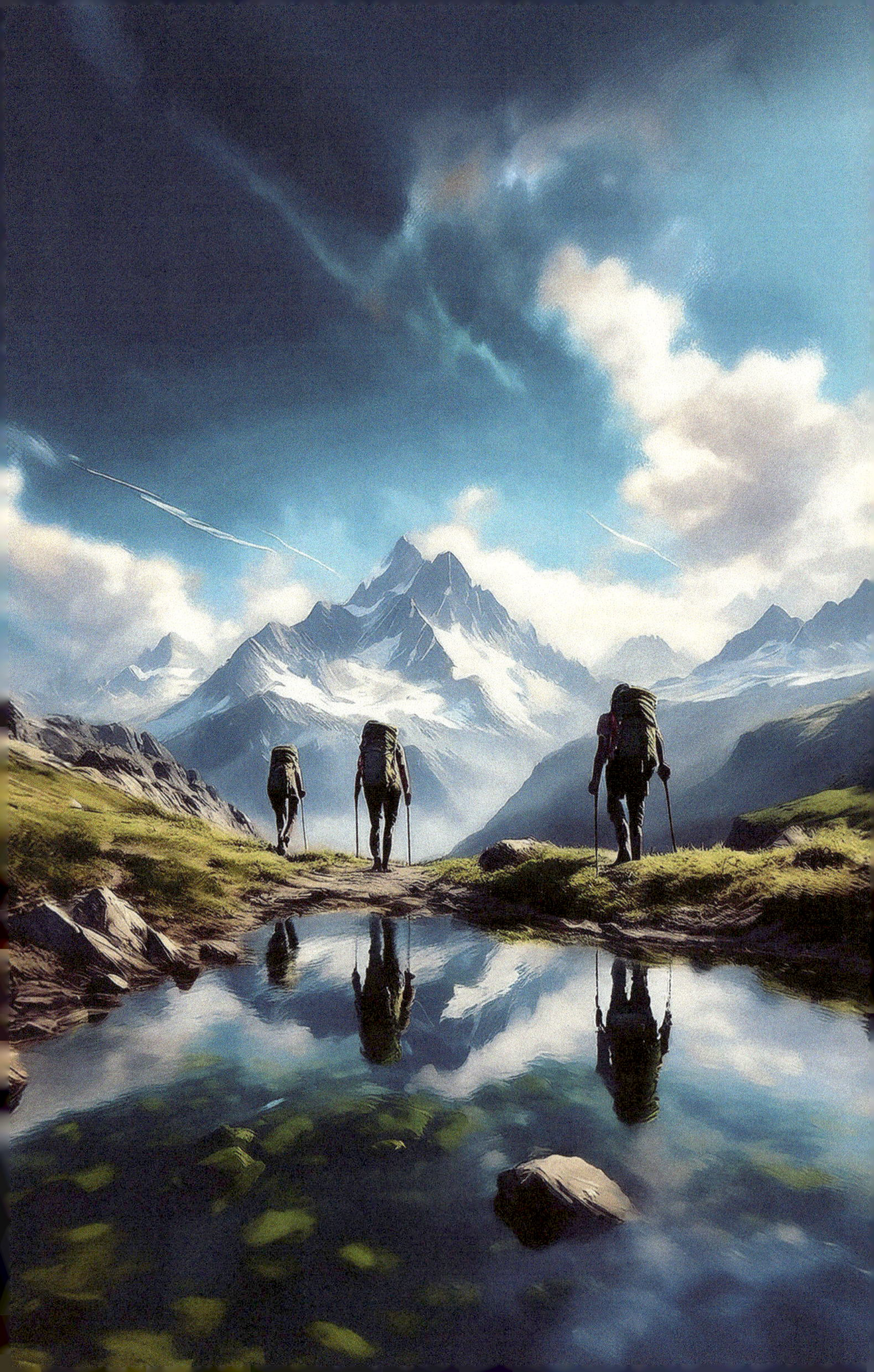

To let it guide you, teach you. It's a gift, one that not everyone is open to receiving."

Tenzin placed a hand on Nat's shoulder, his touch gentle yet powerful. "Remember this feeling. Carry it with you, on every climb and in every moment of your life. The wisdom is always there, the lessons waiting to be learned. All you have to do is listen and trust in the path the mountain sets before you."

With those words echoing in her heart, Nat turned her face to the summit, to the final leg of their climb. But she knew with a bone-deep certainty that the true peak, the true achievement, was already within her grasp. For in opening herself to the mountain, in learning to hear its whispers and heed its signs, she had found something far greater than any physical summit. She had found a way back to herself, a path forward into a future rich with meaning and purpose.

And as they climbed on, Nat felt a profound sense of gratitude, awe, and wonder—for the mountain, for Tenzin and Evie, for the journey that had brought her to this moment.

And for the lessons that awaited her, just beyond the next ridge, the next horizon.

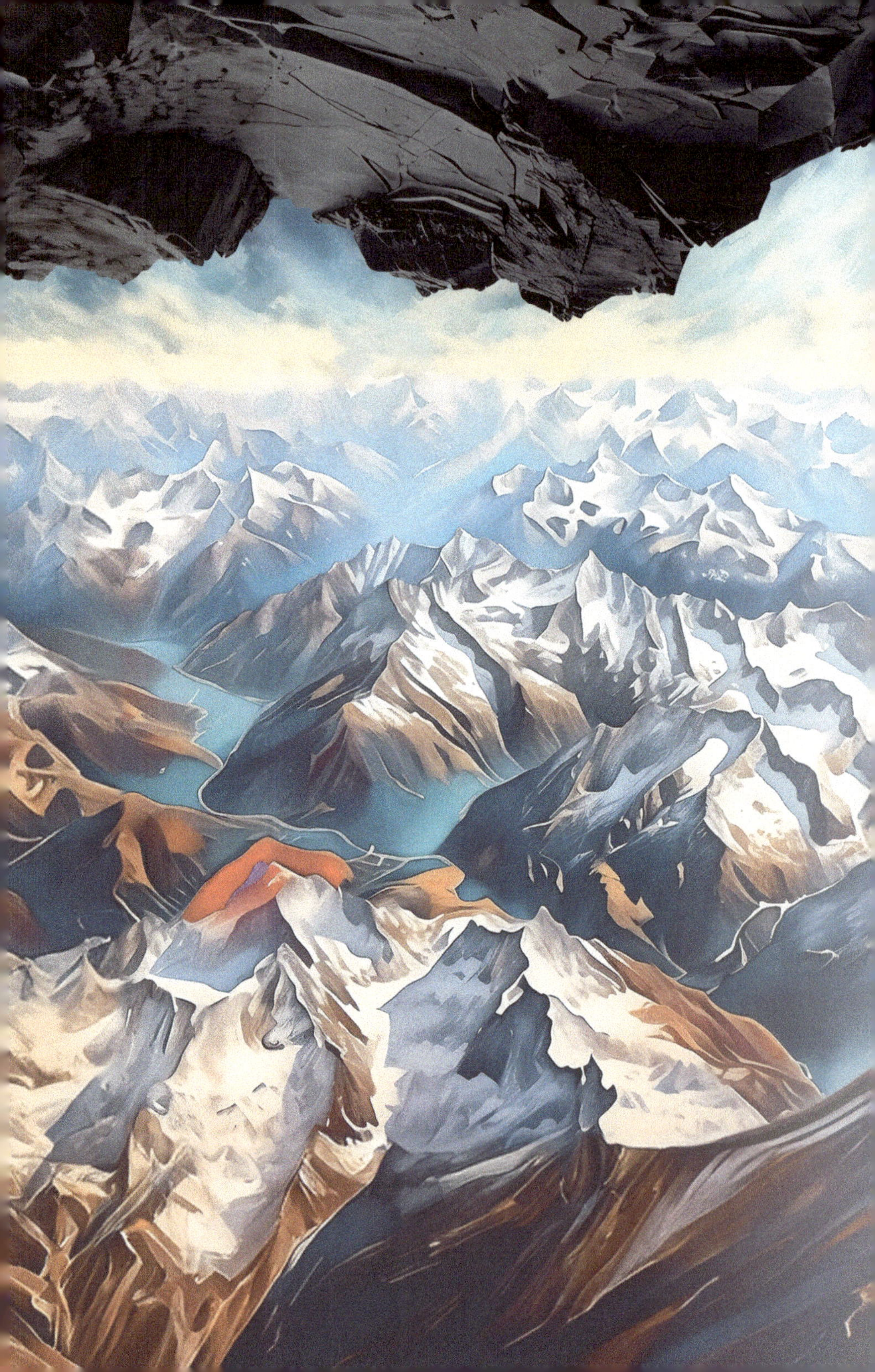

5

Faith Over Fear

• • • •

The journey from the lush green valleys of the Swiss Alps to the stark, unforgiving landscape of the Karakoram was a study in contrasts. Nat and Evie had departed from the small regional airport in Sion, where they boarded a turboprop plane that carried them over the snow-capped peaks and glacial lakes of the Alps.

From there, they had connected through a series of larger airports—Zurich, Dubai, Islamabad—each one a hub of activity and energy, a crossroads of cultures and destinations. The final leg of their journey involved a small chartered plane—the kind used by mountaineers and trekkers to access the most remote reaches of the world.

As they soared over the rugged terrain, the jagged peaks and vast glaciers stretching out to the horizon, Nat turned to Evie, a thoughtful expression on her face. "You know, this expedition feels different than any other I've ever been on."

"I felt the same way when I first embarked on this path, all those years ago," Evie said. "It's like the mountains themselves are calling to you, beckoning you to explore not just their physical heights, but the depths of your own being." She leaned back in her seat, her gaze distant. "I think it's because you're in search of something different now. Not just the thrill of the climb, or the accolades of the summit—but a deeper understanding of yourself and your place in the world. The mountains have a way of stripping away the layers, of revealing the truth that lies beneath. And that can be a powerful and transformative experience, if you're open to it."

Nat thought of all the climbs she had undertaken, all the peaks she had conquered—and how, despite the exhilaration and sense of accomplishment, a tiny part of herself always felt like something was missing. It was as if she had been chasing after something indefinable, some elusive sense of purpose or meaning that always seemed to slip through her grasp. But now, as she sat beside Evie, the vast and wild landscape of the Karakoram unfolding before them, she felt a flicker of hope, of possibility. Maybe this entire journey would be different. Maybe, in the crucible of the mountains, she would find the answers she had been seeking for so long.

Evie, sensing the direction of Nat's thoughts, nudged her with an elbow. "Or maybe you're just ready to admit that I'm the superior climber, and you're hoping to learn from the master."

Nat laughed and nudged Evie back. "In your dreams, old lady."

They dissolved into laughter as the plane began its descent, the tiny mountain village of Hushe appearing like a toy model below them. Nat felt a sense of excitement, of readiness, building within her. Whatever lay ahead, whatever challenges and revelations the mountains had in store, she was ready to meet them head-on.

As Nat stepped off the small prop plane onto the dusty airstrip, her breath caught at the sight before her. The Trango Towers loomed in the distance, their sheer granite faces piercing the brilliant blue sky, daring anyone to take up the challenge they presented.

The following day, they gathered their gear and made the short trek to the small cluster of tents that would serve as their base camp. Nearby, a figure emerged from the shadows of a large boulder—tall and lean, with high cheekbones and almond-shaped eyes that glinted with a fierce intelligence. His hair was long and black, plaited into a neat braid that hung down his back.

"Lhakpa." Evie said, clasping his hand in both of hers. "It's good to see you again, my friend."

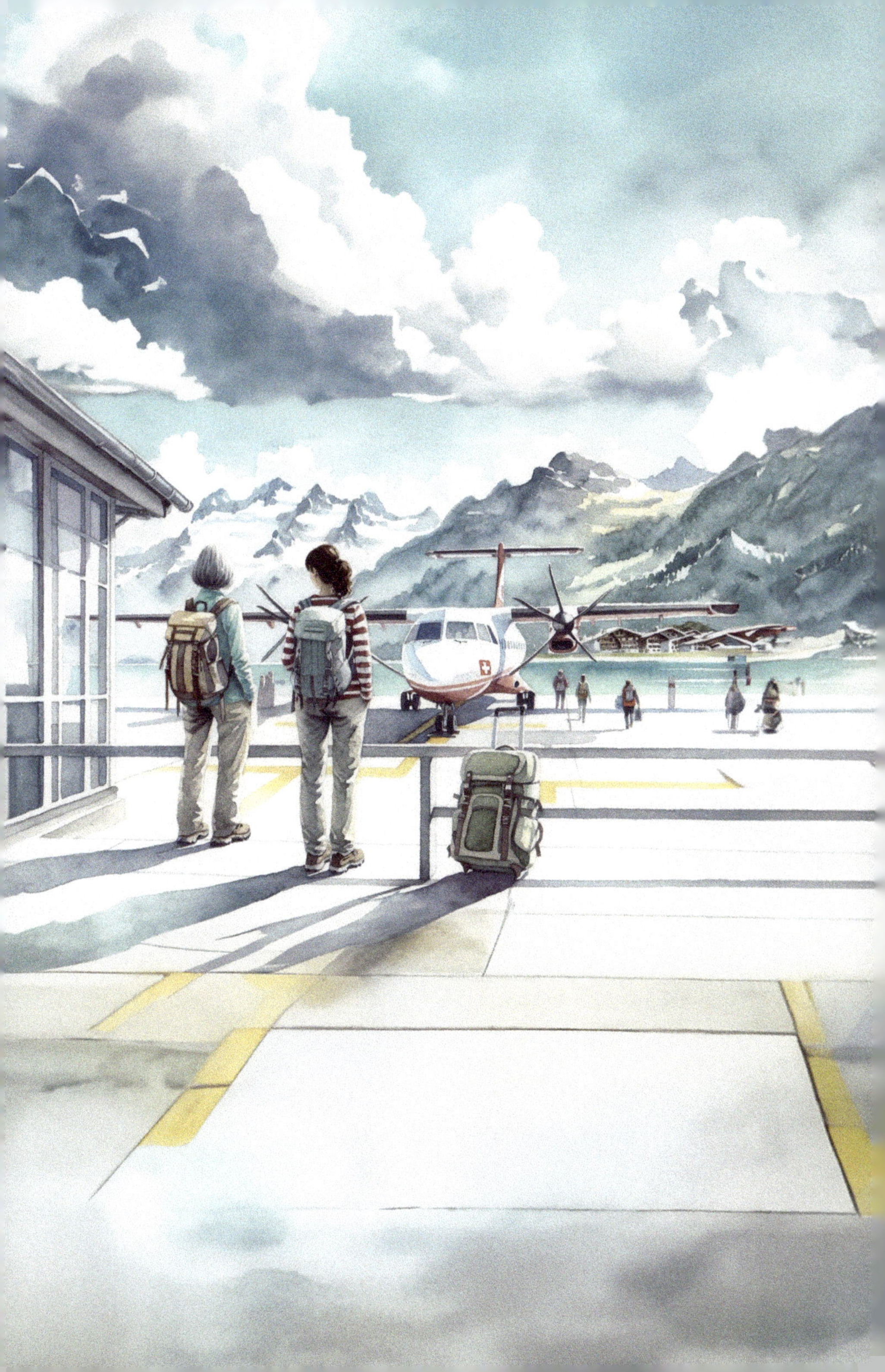

Lhakpa inclined his head, a small smile playing at the corners of his mouth. "Evie. You look well." He turned to Nat, appraising her with a cool gaze. "And you must be Natalia."

Nat felt a flicker of unease under his scrutiny, but she met his eyes steadily. "It's an honor to meet you, Lhakpa. Evie has spoken very highly of you."

Lhakpa's smile widened. He gestured toward the tents, his movements precise and economical. "Come. Let us prepare for the climb. The Towers await."

As they sorted through their gear and double-checked their supplies, Lhakpa spoke, his voice low and measured. "Tell me, Natalia. What do you know of the Trango Towers?"

Nat paused, considering. "They're some of the most challenging peaks in the world. The routes are long and sustained, with sections of blank, featureless rock that require absolute commitment and precision."

Lhakpa nodded, his eyes fixed on the coil of rope he was inspecting. "Yes. The Towers demand much of those who would climb them. But the greatest challenge, the true test, lies not in the rock and ice, but in the mind of the climber. Do you know the story of the young monk and the rope bridge?"

Nat shook her head, intrigued.

Lhakpa settled back on his haunches, his voice taking on the cadence of a well-practiced tale. "Once, in a monastery high in the mountains, there lived a young monk named Phuntsok. Phuntsok was a diligent student, but he was plagued by doubts and fears, always questioning his own abilities and worth. One day, the abbot of the monastery called Phuntsok to him. 'I have a task for you,' the abbot said. 'On the other side of the great chasm that separates our monastery from the world, there is a village in need of our help. You must cross the chasm and deliver this message of hope and compassion.'

"Phuntsok's heart quailed at the thought. The chasm was deep and wide, spanned only by a thin rope bridge that swayed and danced in the wind. 'Master,' he said, his voice trembling, 'I am afraid. The bridge is so narrow, the drop so far. What if I fall?'

"The abbot smiled. 'Phuntsok,' he said, 'the only thing that can make you fall is your own fear. The bridge is narrow, yes, but it is strong. It has carried many before you, and it will carry you now. But you must have faith—in the bridge and in yourself.'

"Once at the chasm, Phuntsok took a deep breath. Then, slowly, he stepped out onto the bridge. At first, his steps were hesitant, his body rigid. But as he focused on the path ahead, on the destination that awaited him, his fear began to fade. With each step, his confidence grew, until he was striding across the chasm with a sure and steady gait.

"And when he reached the other side, when he looked back at the swaying bridge and the dizzying drop below, he realized that the abbot was right. It was not the bridge that had carried him across, but his own faith—his own belief in himself."

Lhakpa fell silent for a moment. "The same is true on the mountain, Natalia. Fear and faith cannot coexist. You must choose one or the other. And if you choose faith, if you trust in your own strength and the support of those around you, there is nothing you cannot accomplish."

Nat fiddled with the zipper of her pack as she pondered his words. How many times had she let fear hold her back, on the rock and in her life? How many opportunities had she missed, how many challenges had she shied away from because she doubted herself?

Evie chimed in from nearby. "I remember when Lhakpa first told me that story on a climb, years ago. I was facing a section of rock that had me trembling with fear, convinced I couldn't do it. But his words, the lesson of the young monk, it changed everything for me. It was like a switch flipped in my mind. I realized that the only thing holding me back was my own fear, my own lack of belief. In that moment, I made the choice to have faith—in myself and in the climb. And suddenly, anything seemed possible."

Nat nodded, absorbing Evie's words. She thought of all the times she had let doubt creep in, let insecurity cloud her judgment. The missed opportunities, the half-hearted attempts. The sense of being stuck, of not living up to her full potential. "I want that," she said, almost to herself. "That kind of faith, that kind of freedom."

Lhakpa smiled, a rare warmth softening his features. "Then let us begin. The Towers will be your teacher. Trust in their lessons and in yourself, and you will find what you seek."

With those words ringing in her ears, Nat shouldered her pack and followed Lhakpa and Evie out of base camp, toward the towering spires of rock looming above them.

As they climbed, Nat felt the old familiar doubts and fears creeping in, whispering in the back of her mind. The rock was steep and unforgiving, the exposure dizzying. More than once, she found herself frozen in place, her muscles locked with tension as she stared down at the yawning void below.

But each time, she heard Lhakpa's calming voice in her head. *Choose faith. Trust in yourself, in the strength of your body and the power of your will.*

And so she did. With each deep breath, each deliberate movement, she pushed through the fear, focusing on the present moment, on the feel of the rock beneath her fingers and the sun on her face. And slowly, inch by inch, she made her way up the mountain, one pitch at a time.

Lhakpa and Evie climbed ahead of her, their movements fluid and graceful. But Nat could feel their attention on her, could sense their quiet encouragement and support. It bolstered her, giving her the courage to keep pushing, keep reaching for the next hold, the next ledge.

At one point, a blank stretch of vertical rock seemed to offer no way forward. Nat felt the old panic rising in her throat. Her hands were slick with sweat, her arms trembling with fatigue. Every instinct screamed at her to back down, to retreat to the safety of the ledge below.

But then she heard Evie's voice drifting down from above. "You've got this, Nat. Trust your feet, trust your hands. The route is there, you just have to believe in it. Believe in yourself."

In that moment, something shifted inside Nat. A flicker of determination, of stubborn will, sparked to life. She took a deep breath, centering herself. With a surge of power and purpose, she pushed upward, her fingers seeking the tiniest of holds, her feet taking advantage of the rock's faintest contours.

It was a dance, a delicate balance of strength and finesse. And as she glided up the rock, Nat was overcome with exhilaration. She was meant for this. She was born for it. Not for the summit, not the accolades or the adrenaline rush, but the climb itself—the perfect union of body and mind, of will and rock.

SURVIVING GREATNESS

As she pulled herself over the final ledge and stood atop the spire with Lhakpa and Evie, the world spread out below her like a canvas, Nat felt a sense of profound gratitude, of humility and awe. Looking out over the sprawling expanse of peaks and valleys, at the play of light and shadow on the ancient stone, she knew she would carry this moment with her always—this lesson of faith and fearlessness.

Evie grinned, slinging an arm around Nat's shoulders. "I'm proud of you, kiddo. You faced your fears head-on today, and you came out stronger for it. That's the real summit."

"I couldn't have done it without you," Nat said. "Without both of you."

Lhakpa inclined his head. "We are all students on the mountain, Natalia. We all have much to learn, and much to teach. The key is to remain open, to keep seeking and striving, even in the face of fear and doubt. But there is another lesson, one that is often overlooked. Sometimes, to find clarity and see the path ahead, we must first learn to let go."

Nat frowned, puzzled by his words. "Let go? What do you mean?"

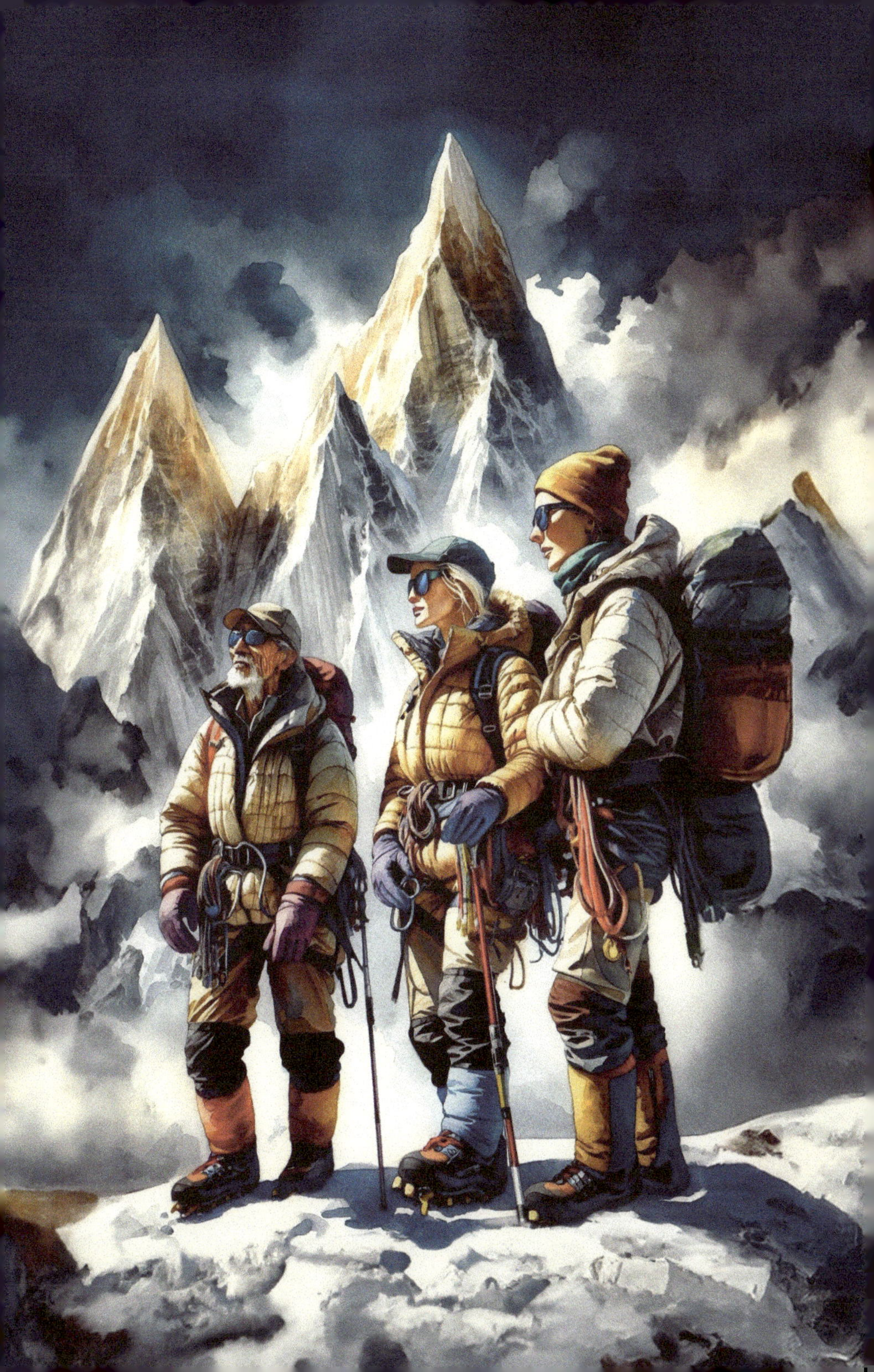

"So often in life," Lhakpa continued, "we cling to the illusion of control. We grip tightly our plans, our expectations, our fears. We believe that by holding on, we can somehow shape the outcome, bend the world to our will." He shook his head. "But the mountain, she teaches us a different way. She shows us that true strength, true clarity, comes not from grasping, but from surrendering. From letting go of our preconceptions, our attachments, and trusting in the path as it unfolds."

"But how do we let go, when everything in us wants to hold on?" Nat said.

Lhakpa reached out, placing a hand on her shoulder. His touch was firm, grounding. "By remembering that we are not in control. Not really. The mountain, the weather, the very forces of nature—they are far greater than us, far beyond our ability to dictate or command. When we let go, when we surrender to that truth, we open ourselves up to a different kind of power. The power of acceptance, of trust, of flow. We find our way forward not by resisting, but by yielding."

"Let go," Nat murmured, testing the phrase on her tongue. "Surrender to the path."

As they picked their way down the mountain's flanks with the sun edging closer to the horizon, Nat felt a sense of peace, of purpose, settling over her like a mantle. The true journey, the real adventure, was not in the destination, but in the climb itself. In the choices she made, moment by moment. In her faith, her ability to trust herself, and in the letting go of her fears and expectations, allowing the path to unfold before her.

With that knowledge, she knew she could face anything—both on the mountain and in life.

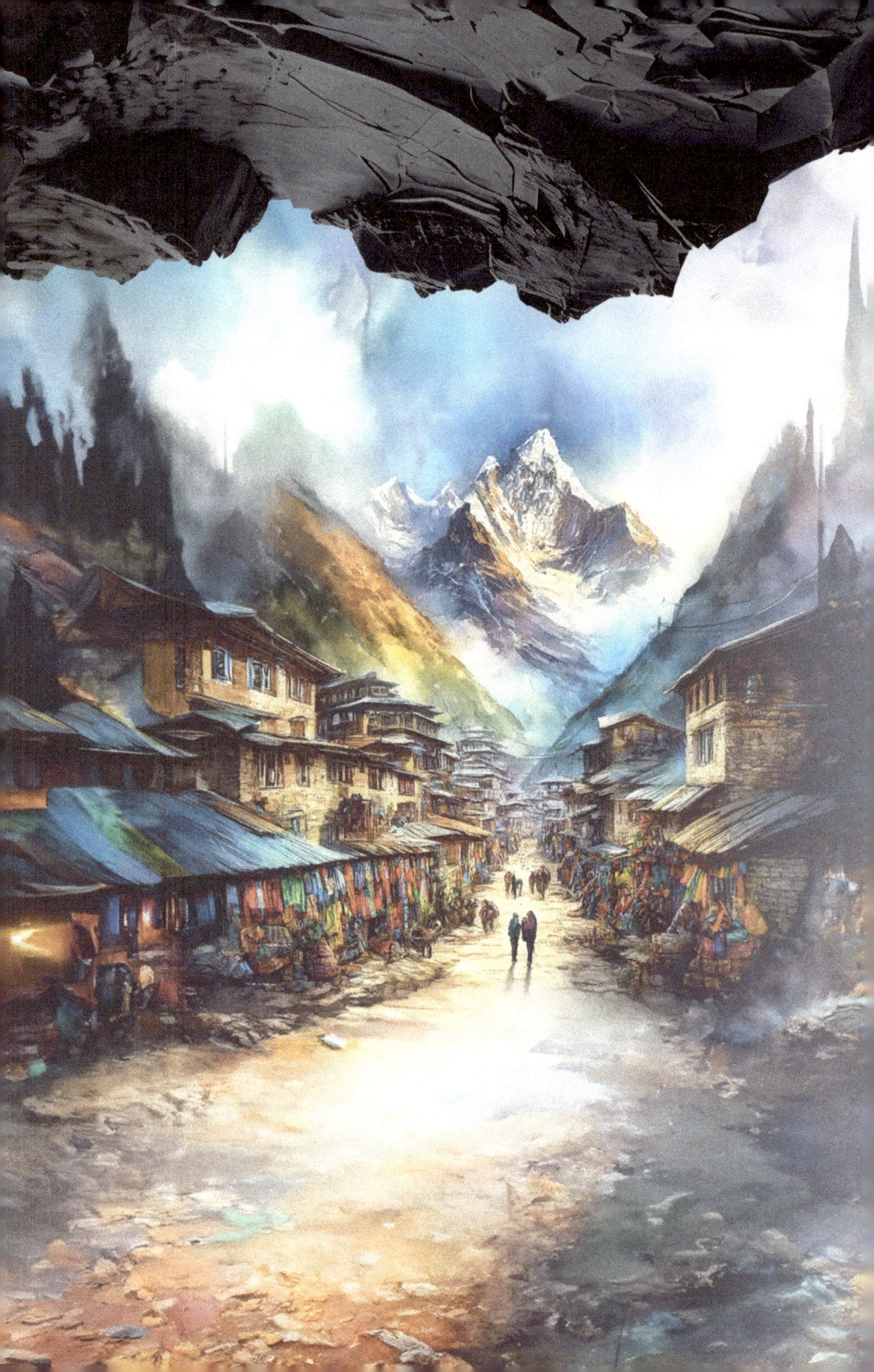

6 Readiness is a Choice

• ● ● ● •

The village of Pangboche was a kaleidoscope of vibrant colors and lively sounds, a bustling hub of activity nestled in the shadow of Ama Dablam's majestic peak. As Nat and Evie walked through the narrow, winding streets, they were greeted by the warm smiles and friendly waves of the locals, their weathered faces etched with the lines of a life lived in harmony with the mountains. The air was filled with the aroma of spices and the chatter of voices, a symphony of life and energy that seemed to pulse with the very heartbeat of the Himalayas.

SURVIVING GREATNESS

Leading the way was Dawa, a petite Nepali woman with a quick smile and a mischievous glint in her eye. She moved through the village with the easy grace of someone who had called these hills home for a lifetime, stopping now and then to exchange a few words with a passing friend or to point out a particularly stunning vista. Her laughter rang out like a bell, infectious and joyful, and Nat found herself smiling in response, drawn in by Dawa's irrepressible spirit.

As they began their ascent of Ama Dablam's lower slopes, Dawa kept up a steady stream of encouragement and insight, her words drifting back to Nat on the thin mountain air. "The mountain is a great teacher," she said. "It has so much to show us, if we are willing to be present—to listen and learn."

Nat focused on the rhythm of her breathing and the placement of her feet, finding a sense of flow in the physical demands of the climb. The trail was steep and rocky, winding its way up through a landscape of stunning beauty and rugged grandeur. The air grew thinner as they climbed, and Nat felt her lungs burning with the effort. Yet she pushed on, determined to rise to the challenge.

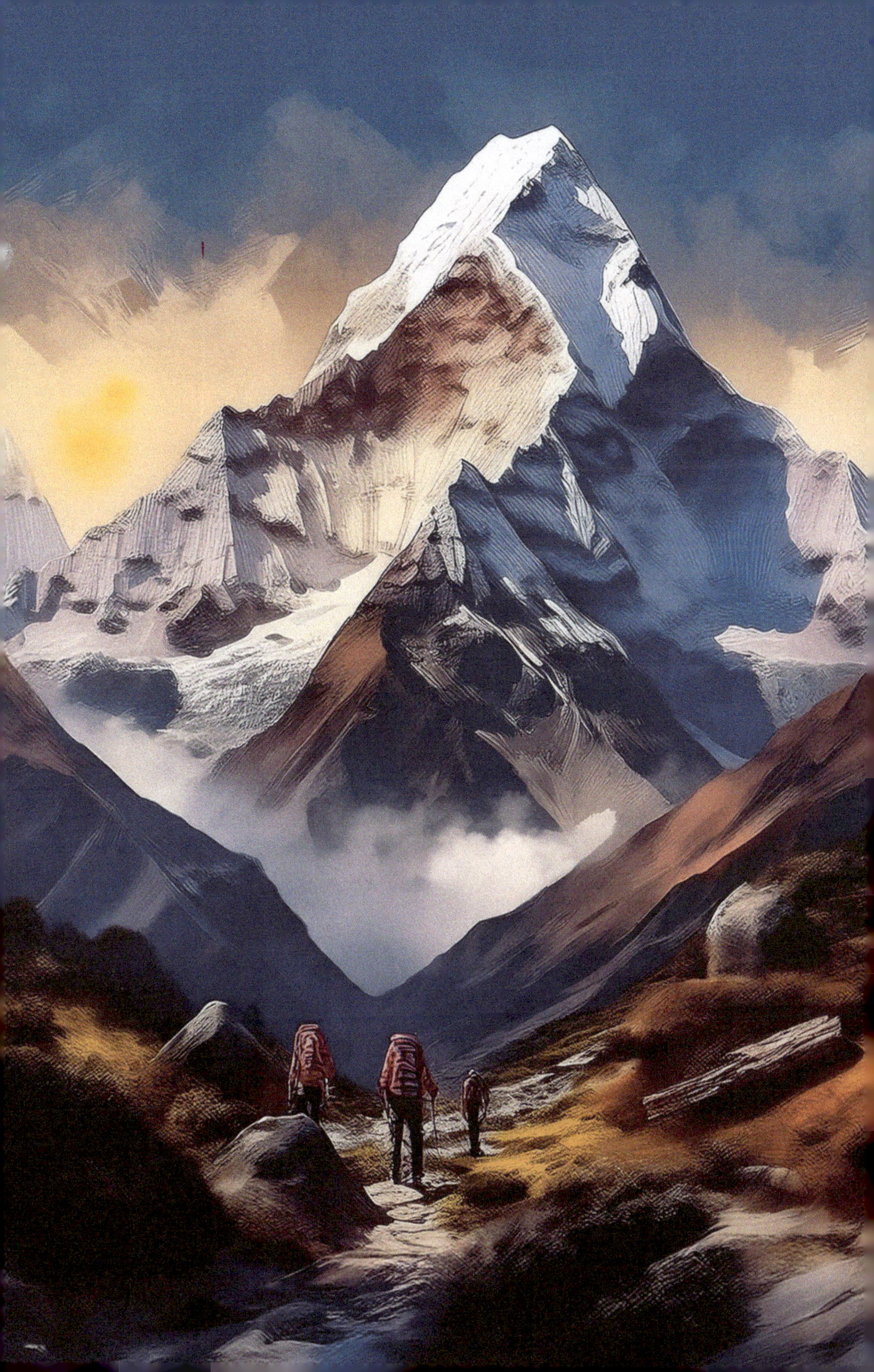

However, as they approached a challenging section of the route—a sheer rock face with few apparent handholds—Nat felt a flicker of doubt. The wall loomed before her, seeming to mock her with its unyielding surface. Her palms grew slick with sweat as she searched for a way up.

Dawa, sensing Nat's hesitation, paused and turned to face her. Her eyes were warm and understanding, but there was a firmness in her gaze that commanded attention. "You know, there's a saying in my village. 'The mountain doesn't care if you're ready. It's waiting for you to decide that you're ready.'"

Nat frowned, puzzled by Dawa's words. She had always thought of readiness as a feeling, a state of being that one either possessed or didn't. The idea that it could be a choice, a decision to be made, was new to her. "What do you mean?"

Dawa settled herself on a nearby rock. She patted the space beside her, inviting Nat to join her. "Let me tell you a story. When I was a young girl, just starting to learn the ways of the mountain, I came across a climb that filled me with fear. It was a route I had never attempted before, and the thought of it made my heart race and my mind fill with doubt. If I had never done it before, how could I know I would be successful?"

She paused, letting the silence stretch out for a long moment. Nat could almost see the young Dawa in her mind's eye, standing at the base of that climb, her face etched with uncertainty.

"I waited at the base of that climb for hours," Dawa continued. "I told myself I would start when I felt ready, when the fear had passed and I was filled with confidence and strength. But the feeling never came. The more I waited, the more my fear grew, until it seemed an insurmountable obstacle in itself."

Nat nodded, recognizing the sensation all too well. How many times had she found herself paralyzed by doubt, waiting for a sense of readiness that remained maddeningly elusive? It was a trap she had fallen into many times—and not just when climbing.

"It was my mentor," Dawa said, "a wise old Sherpa named Dorje, who finally shook me out of my stupor. He came upon me there, huddled at the base of the climb, and asked what I was waiting for. When I told him I was waiting to feel ready, he laughed out loud." She shook her head, smiling at the memory.

"'Dawa,' he said, 'being ready is not a feeling. It's a decision. You will never feel fully prepared for the challenges the mountain—or life—presents. But you can choose, in each moment, to face those challenges with courage and resolve. That is the true definition of greatness.'"

"Dorje's words ring true," Evie added. "Not just for climbing, but for life itself. We often wait for the perfect moment, the perfect set of circumstances, before we take action. We tell ourselves we'll start that project when we have more time, or pursue that dream when we feel more confident. But the reality is, that perfect moment may never come. It's up to us to create it, to decide that we are ready, even in the face of fear and uncertainty.

"Think about your own life, Nat—when you held yourself back, waiting for a sign that you were ready to take the next step. Whether it was in your climbing career or in your personal life, I bet there were moments when you felt paralyzed by doubt, unable to move forward because you didn't feel fully prepared."

Evie's words hit close to home, echoing the struggles and doubts that had plagued Nat for so long. How often had she let her own fears dictate her actions, holding her back from taking the very leaps that promised the greatest growth and fulfillment?

Dawa stood, dusting off her hands. She fixed Nat with a gaze that was at once compassionate and challenging. "From that day forward, I began to approach each climb, each challenge, with a new perspective. I learned to recognize my fear, to acknowledge its presence—and then to choose to act despite it. And with each choice, each decision to move forward, I felt my confidence grow, my sense of what was possible expand. And so, the question before you now is not whether you feel ready to face this climb, but whether you *choose* to be ready. Whether you decide to lean into the discomfort, to embrace the challenge, and to trust in your own strength and resilience to carry you through."

Nat took a deep breath, feeling the truth of Dawa's words settle into her bones. She thought of all the times she had let her doubts hold her back, all the opportunities for growth and learning she had missed out on because she was waiting for a feeling that never came. The realization was like a lightning bolt, illuminating the patterns and habits that had kept her stuck for so long.

But now, standing at the base of this daunting climb, she realized that the power to move forward had been within her all along. That readiness was not some external state to be achieved, but an internal commitment to be made, again and again, when faced with fear and uncertainty.

With a nod of determination, Nat stepped forward, her gaze fixed on the rock face before her. She took a deep breath, centering herself in the present moment—and then, with a surge of resolve, she began to climb.

As she navigated the challenging holds and precarious footholds, Nat felt a new sense of clarity and focus take hold. Yes, the climb was difficult—more difficult than most anything she had faced before. But with each move, each decision to continue upward, she felt her confidence grow, her sense of her own capability deepen.

The rock was rough and unyielding beneath her fingers, and the exposure was dizzying, the void yawning beneath her feet. But Nat pushed on, her breath coming in sharp, focused bursts, her mind utterly absorbed in the flow of the climb. She felt a sense of oneness with the mountain, a deep connection to the primal forces of nature that shaped and tested her with every move.

And when at last she pulled herself over the final ledge, her muscles trembling with exertion and her heart pounding with exhilaration, she felt a swell of accomplishment wash over her. Not just for the completion of the climb itself, but for the internal shift that had taken place, the decision she had made to embrace readiness as a choice rather than a feeling.

Dawa and Evie, who had followed close behind, grinned with pride as they joined Nat on the ledge. Dawa pulled Nat into a fierce hug, her eyes shining. "You did it! You chose to be ready and faced your fear. That takes a special kind of courage, a willingness to step into the unknown and trust in your own strength."

"And that's a lesson you can carry with you, Nat," Evie said. "In every aspect of your life. Whenever you face a challenge, a decision, a moment of uncertainty—remember that readiness is a choice. That you have the power to decide how you will meet that challenge, how you will show up and move forward."

Nat looked out at the vast expanse of the Himalayas, the jagged peaks and glacial valleys stretching out to the horizon, and felt a sense of deep connection to the wild and untamed beauty of the landscape. "I think I'm starting to understand. All this time, I've been waiting for some external validation, some sign that I was ready for the next step, the next challenge. I've been looking for permission, for someone else to tell me I was capable and worthy. But the truth is, that validation, that readiness—it comes from within. It's a decision I make." She paused as the realization dawned on her. "I'm the one I've been waiting for."

"You are indeed," Dawa said. "And with each decision, each choice to step forward into the unknown—you become more fully yourself, more aligned with your own strength and potential. The mountain, and life itself, will always present new challenges, new opportunities to stretch and grow. But if you can meet those challenges with a spirit of readiness, of willingness to embrace the discomfort and the uncertainty—then there is no limit to what you can achieve, no summit beyond your reach."

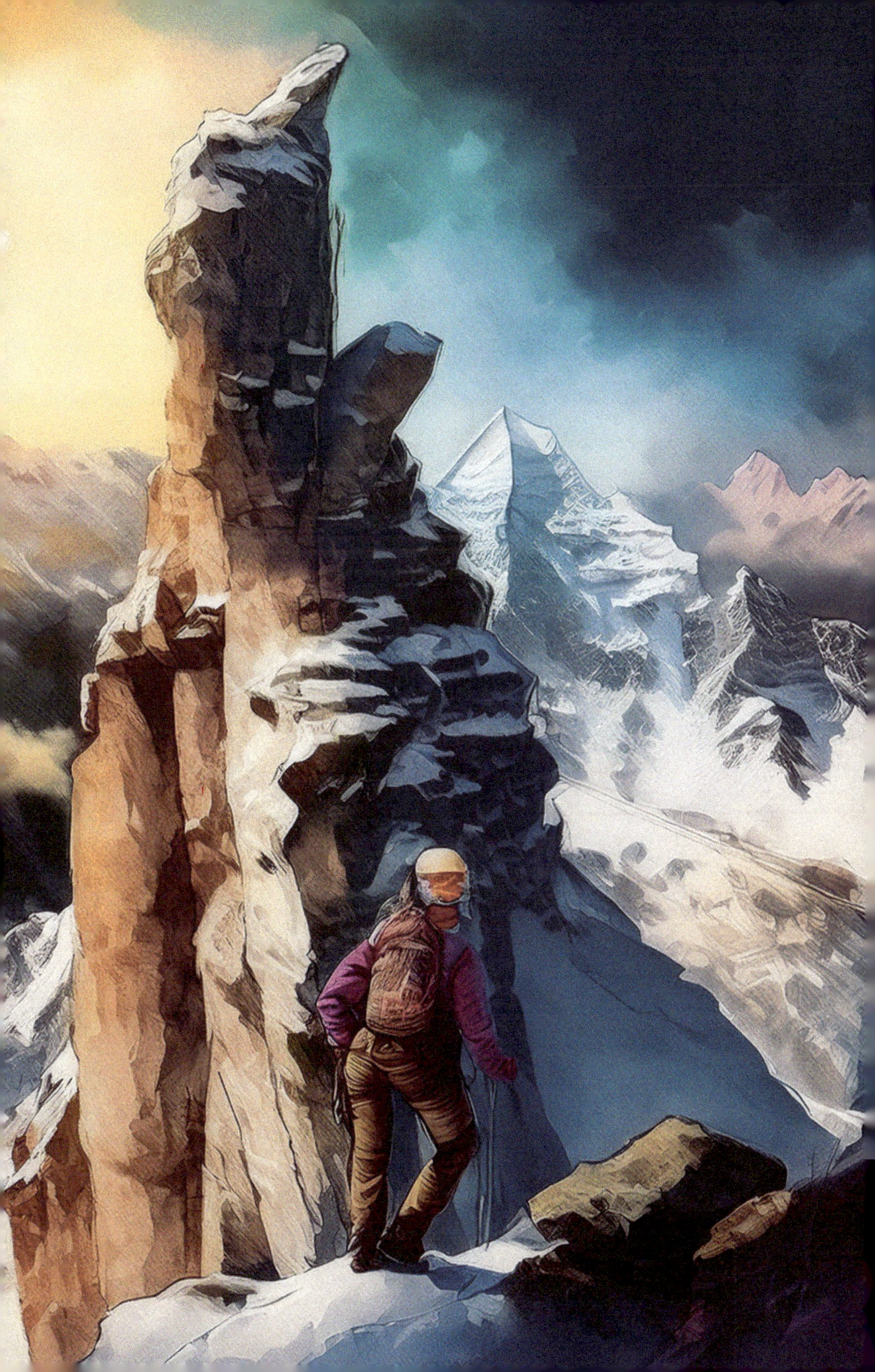

Evie smiled. "It's a beautiful thing, to watch you step into your own power. You've grown so much on this journey—not just as a climber, but as a person. You've faced your fears, your doubts, your limitations—and you've chosen, again and again, to rise above them. That takes a special kind of courage, a deep trust in yourself and your own path."

Nat felt a wave of emotion that threatened to overwhelm her. She thought of all the challenges she had faced, all the moments of fear and uncertainty and self-doubt. And she realized that each of those moments had been an opportunity, a chance to choose readiness, to step forward into growth and transformation.

"Thank you," she said, her voice thick. "Thank you, both. I feel like I'm seeing the world, and myself, through fresh eyes. Like I'm ready for whatever's next in a way I've never been before."

"That's the spirit!" Dawa said. "The mountain is calling, and you are ready to answer. So let's climb on and see what other lessons and wonders await us on this path."

They turned their faces to the sun, to the vast and beckoning expanse of the Himalayas. Nat felt a sense of peace and purpose settle over her. She had learned, on the steep and rugged flanks of Ama Dablam, that true readiness came not from external circumstances, but from an internal commitment, a willingness to step forward into the unknown with courage and resolve.

And with that commitment, that choice to embrace the challenge and the growth that lay ahead, she knew that anything was possible—on the mountain, and in the grand adventure of life itself.

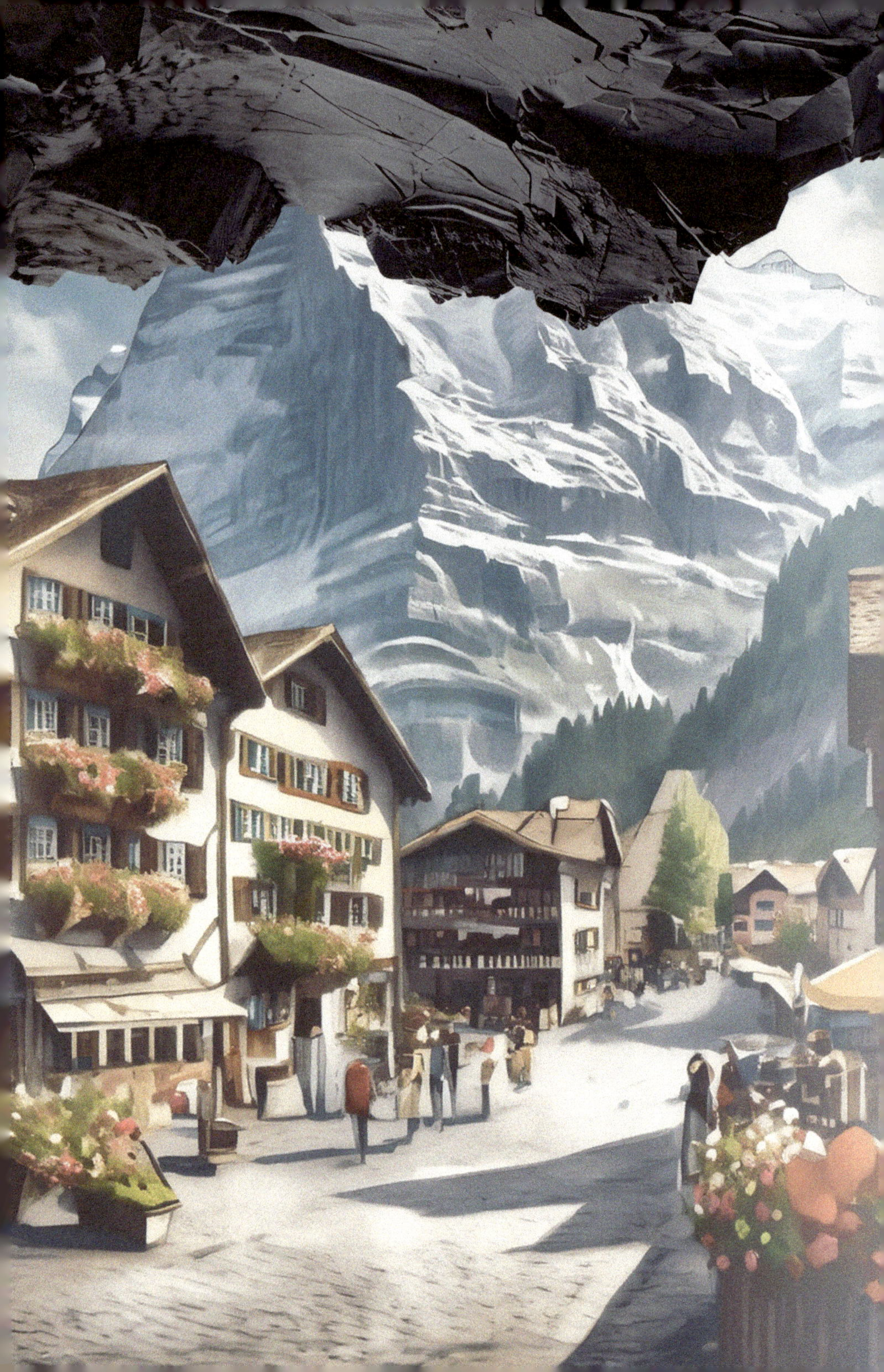

7

Obstacles as Growth Catalysts

• • • • •

The train ride from the bustling streets of Interlaken to the quieter, more rustic village of Grindelwald, Switzerland, was a journey back in time, a passage into a world where the mountains reigned supreme. As Nat stepped onto the platform, the crisp Alpine air filled her lungs. She was back where she had faced some of her greatest challenges and triumphs as a climber.

Beside her, Evie stretched, rolling her shoulders to loosen the stiffness from the long journey. "Ah, the Eiger. She's a formidable lady, but she's got a special place in my heart."

Nat nodded, her eyes drawn to the looming bulk of the mountain in the distance. The Eiger's North Wall, called Nordwand, was a legend of the climbing world—nearly six thousand feet of sheer rock and ice. It had claimed the lives of many brave souls over the years, earning it the ominous nickname Mordwand—the murder wall.

As they made their way through the village, past the traditional wooden chalets with their flower-laden window boxes, Nat's mind drifted back to her own first encounter with the Eiger, several years before. She'd been young and brash then, eager to prove herself against one of the most daunting challenges in the Alps. The climb was grueling, a test of endurance and willpower that pushed her to the very limits of her abilities. There were moments, high on that unforgiving face, when she had questioned her own sanity, wondering what madness had driven her to pit herself against such an implacable foe.

But she had persevered, digging deep into reserves of strength and determination she didn't know she possessed. And when she finally dragged herself over the summit ridge, exhausted and elated in equal measure, she knew the Eiger would forever hold a special place in her heart.

Lost in her memories, Nat almost ran straight into a man who had suddenly appeared on the path before them. He was short and wiry, with a weathered face that spoke of a lifetime spent in the high places of the world. But his eyes were kind, full of a warmth and humor that immediately put Nat at ease.

"Mingma!" Evie exclaimed, stepping forward to embrace the man. "It's so good to see you, old friend."

Their Sherpa for this climb returned the hug with a gentle squeeze. "Evie, Evie! It's been too long." He turned to Nat. "And you must be Natalia. I've heard great things about you. It's an honor to climb with you."

Nat ducked her head, feeling a rush at the compliment. "The honor is mine, Mingma. I've been looking forward to learning from you."

"Ah, but the mountain, she is the true teacher. We are all just students in her classroom."

As they fell into step beside him, making their way toward the base of the climb, Nat studied Mingma's face, trying to read the secrets behind his enigmatic smile. He had a reputation as one of the wisest and most experienced guides in the Himalayas, a man who had seen and done things most climbers could only dream of.

Sensing her gaze, Mingma glanced over at her. "Something on your mind, Natalia?"

Nat hesitated, trying to find the right words. "I was just thinking. The last time I climbed the Eiger, it was one of the hardest things I'd ever done. Physically, mentally, emotionally. I'm not sure I've ever faced a greater challenge."

Mingma hummed thoughtfully, his eyes distant. "Challenge. Obstacle. These are words we use, labels we give to the things that stand in our way. But the mountain, she does not see it that way. To her, there is no such thing as an obstacle. There is only the path. And every step, every struggle, every moment of doubt and fear, these are not enemies to be conquered, but teachers to be learned from."

"I remember when you first told me that, Mingma," Evie said. "It was my first time climbing the Eiger, and I was terrified. I kept looking up at that massive wall of rock and ice, and all I could see was an impossible barrier. But you just smiled that little smile of yours and said, 'Evie, the mountain is not your enemy. She is your friend, your teacher. Embrace what she has to offer, and you will find the strength you need.'"

Mingma grinned. "And did you find the strength?"

"Eventually, yes," Evie replied. "But not before a lot of cursing and crying and wondering what the hell I'd gotten myself into."

The trio laughed as they pushed onward, taking a leisurely pace to reach the base of Nordwand a few hours later. After a rest and some preparation, they began their ascent, and soon Nat felt the familiar rhythm of the climb settle over her. The steady in and out of breath, the crunch of boots on snow and rock, the quiet camaraderie of the rope team moving in sync. But even as her body settled into the physical demands of the task, her mind was whirling, grappling with the enormity of what lay ahead.

The higher they climbed, the more the mountain seemed to loom over them, a vast and impassive presence that dwarfed their tiny human forms. The rock grew steeper, the ice more treacherous, and Nat felt the first stirrings of doubt begin to creep in, the whispers that said she wasn't strong enough or brave enough to face this challenge.

But then Mingma's voice would drift back to her on the wind, a gentle reminder to stay present, to focus on the moment at hand. "One step at a time, Natalia," he would call, his tone light and encouraging. "The summit, it will come. For now, just breathe—just be."

And so she did, letting the mountain teach her, one obstacle at a time. When a tricky section of mixed climbing had her heart pounding and her palms sweating, she leaned into the fear, embracing it as a sign that she was growing, learning.

A sudden storm blew in, pelting them with wind and snow, forcing them to hunker down in a cramped bivouac for hours. Nat used the time to rest, recharge, and visualize the moves she would need to make when the weather cleared.

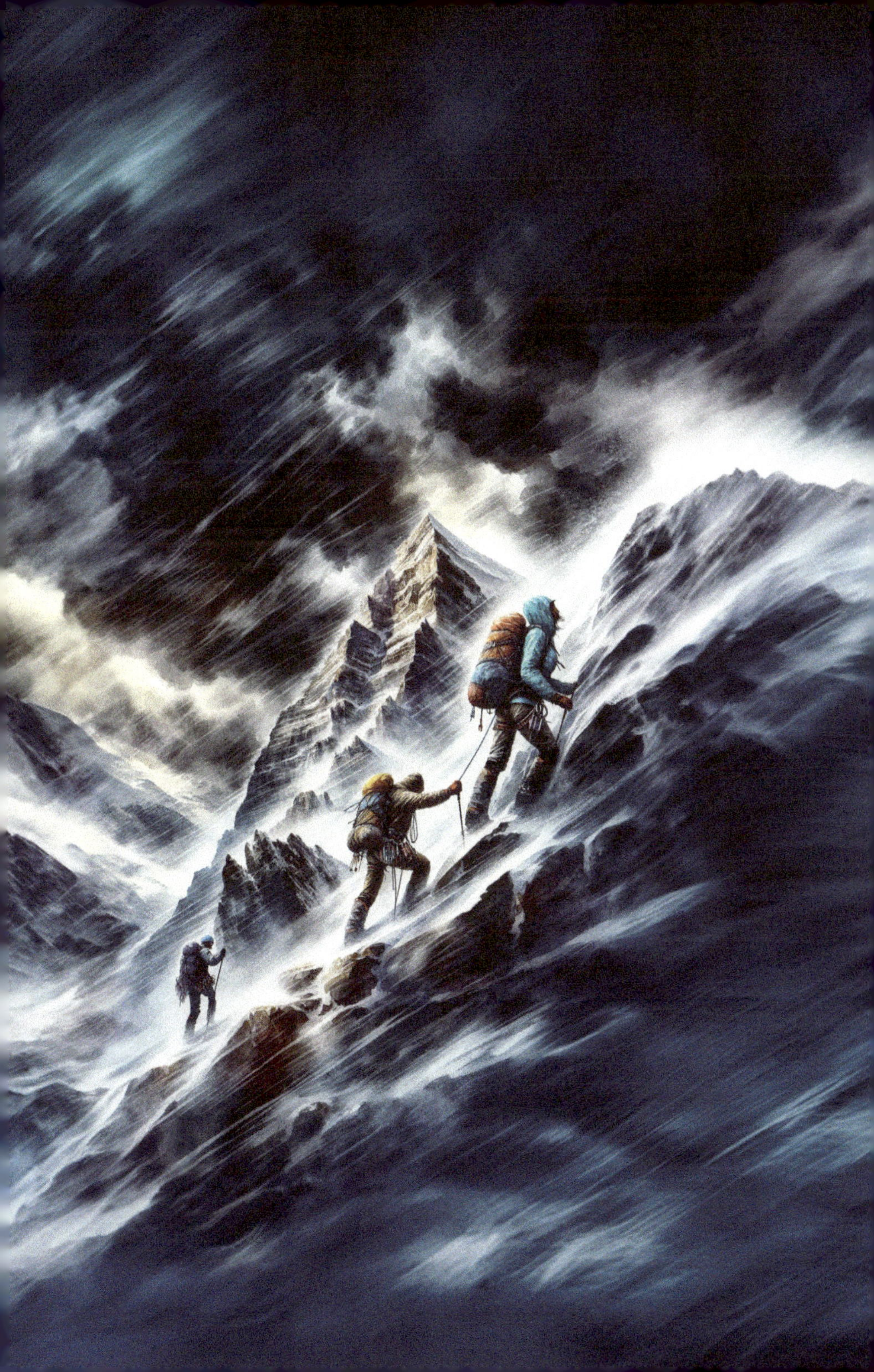

SURVIVING GREATNESS

After the storm, when a harrowing traverse had her questioning her right to be on this mountain, she thought back to a moment years before, when an injury had nearly ended her climbing career before it had even begun.

"I was on a training climb," she told Mingma and Evie as they paused for a breather. "Nothing too crazy, just a local crag I'd done a hundred times before. But I was distracted, not fully present. I missed a hold, and I fell. It was a bad one. Shattered my ankle, tore up my knee pretty good. The doctors said I might never climb again."

Mingma clicked his tongue. "A difficult moment, no doubt. But also, perhaps, an opportunity?"

Nat nodded, a small smile tugging at the corners of her mouth. "It took me a while to see it that way. At first, all I could focus on was what I had lost, the dream that had been taken from me. But as I went through the rehab, the long and painful process of learning to walk again, to move again, something shifted." She looked out at the sweeping vista of the Alps, the jagged peaks and glittering glaciers stretching out to the horizon. "I realized that the injury, as much as it sucked, had also given me a gift. The gift of perspective, of appreciation for what I had. And the drive to come back stronger, to use the setback as fuel for my own growth and development."

"I know that feeling," Evie said. "I've had my share of moments that felt like the end of the road. But each one, in its own way, taught me something valuable. About myself, about the world, about what truly matters."

Mingma's eyes were distant with memory. "There was a climber I knew, many years ago. A prodigy, a true talent. He had the strength, the skill, the burning desire to be the best. But he lacked something essential. Humility. The ability to learn from his mistakes—to see setbacks not as failures, but as opportunities for growth." The old Sherpa shook his head. "He pushed himself too hard, too fast. Refused to listen to his body, to the mountain, to those who cared for him. And in the end, it cost him dearly."

Nat felt a chill run through her, a visceral reminder of the risks they all took in pursuing this calling. But she also felt a flicker of recognition, a sense of kinship with the climber in Mingma's tale. How many times had she pushed herself past the point of reason, past the point of safety, in the single-minded pursuit of a goal? How many warning signs had she ignored? How many voices of caution had she silenced in her own head?

But now, here on the flanks of the Eiger, with the wisdom of Mingma and Evie to guide her, Nat felt a shift within her. A realization that the true summit, the true achievement, lay not in conquering the mountain, but in conquering herself. In learning to listen, to adapt, to grow in the face of adversity.

In the days that followed, as they inched their way up the Nordwand, Nat felt this realization deepen and expand within her. Each challenge, each moment of doubt or fear, became an opportunity to put Mingma's teachings into practice. To embrace the obstacles as teachers—to find the lesson and the growth in every struggle.

And when at last they stood upon the summit, the whole of the Alps spread out below them in a dazzling sea of white, Nat basked in gratitude—for the mountain, with its stern and uncompromising lessons. And for Mingma and Evie, for their patience, their wisdom, their unwavering belief in her.

And gratitude for herself, for the strength and resilience she had found within—for the obstacles she had faced and the person she had become in the process.

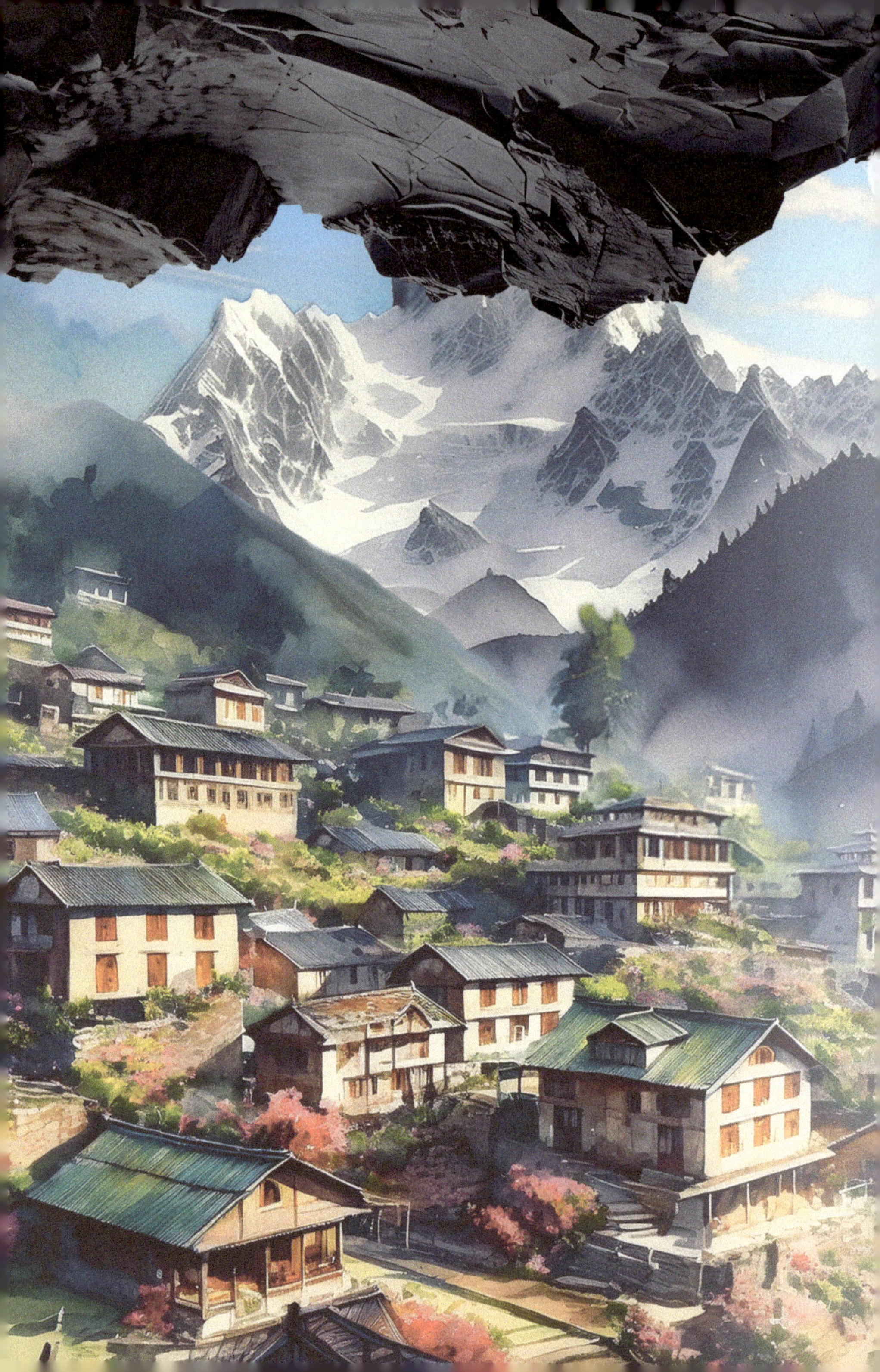

8 The Power of Ritual

• • • •

The journey from the Swiss Alps back to Nepal was a whirlwind of airports, layovers, and jetlag. But as Nat and Evie stepped off the small plane onto the tarmac in Lukla, the gateway to the Khumbu region, Nat felt a sense of coming home. The crisp mountain air filled her lungs, and the distant peaks of the Himalayas beckoned on the horizon.

They made their way to the village of Khumjung, a cluster of stone houses and tea shops nestled in the shadow of Mount Thamserku. The village was a hub of activity, with trekkers and climbers from all over the world passing through on their way to the higher reaches of the Khumbu.

As they walked through the narrow streets, Evie pointed out a small, unassuming temple on the outskirts of the village. "That's where we'll find Sonam. He's an old friend, and one of the wisest people I know."

Inside the temple, they found Sonam, a tall, slender man with weathered skin and a serene expression. He was engaged in a graceful, meditative movement, his body flowing through a series of fluid poses.

When Sonam finished his practice, he turned to greet them, his face breaking into a warm smile. "Evie, my dear friend," he said, embracing her. "And you must be Nat. Welcome to Khumjung. Evie sent word that you are on a great journey. One that tests not only your physical strength and skill, but your mental and emotional fortitude as well. The key to both lies in cultivating presence and focus. And

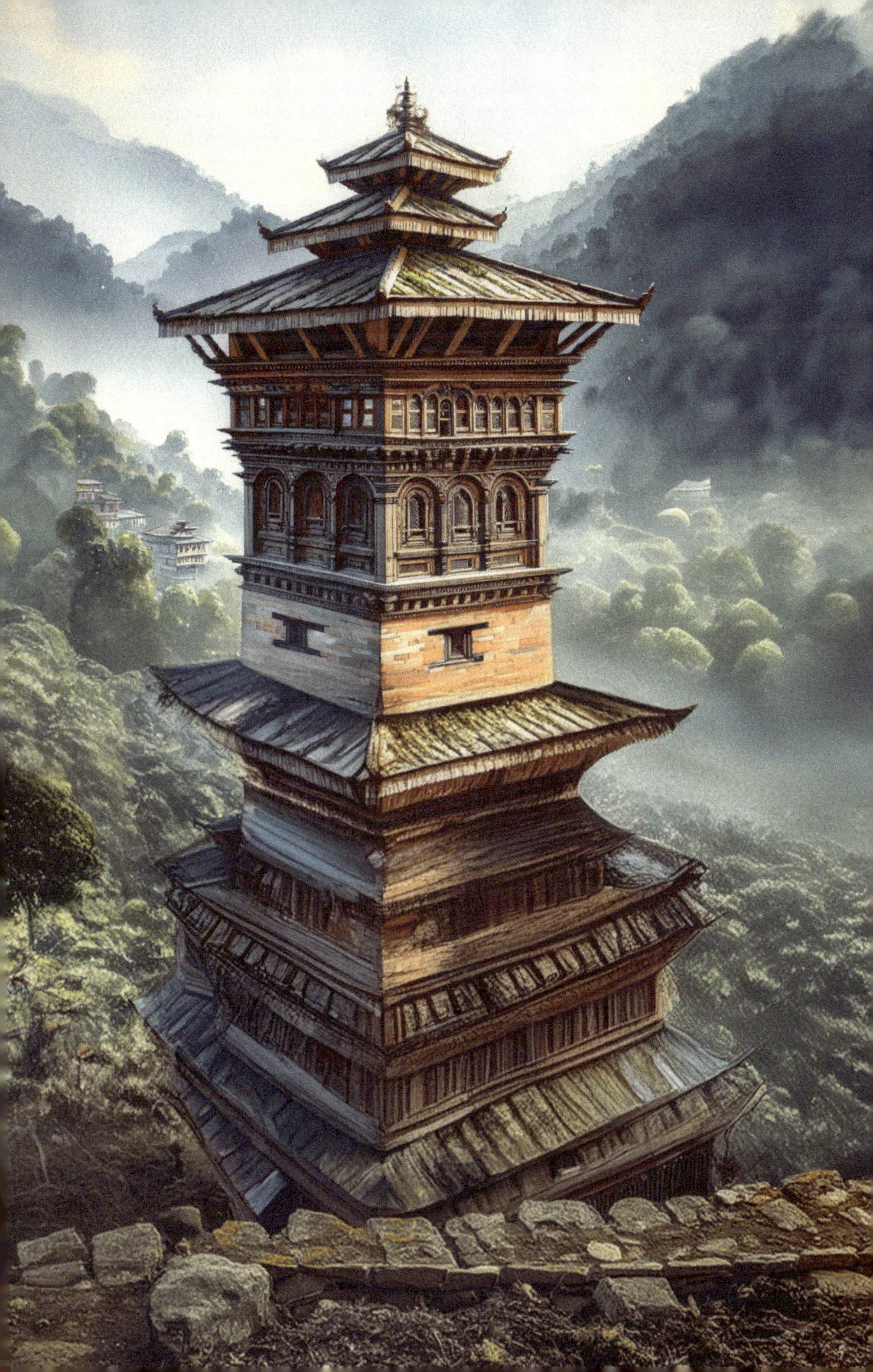

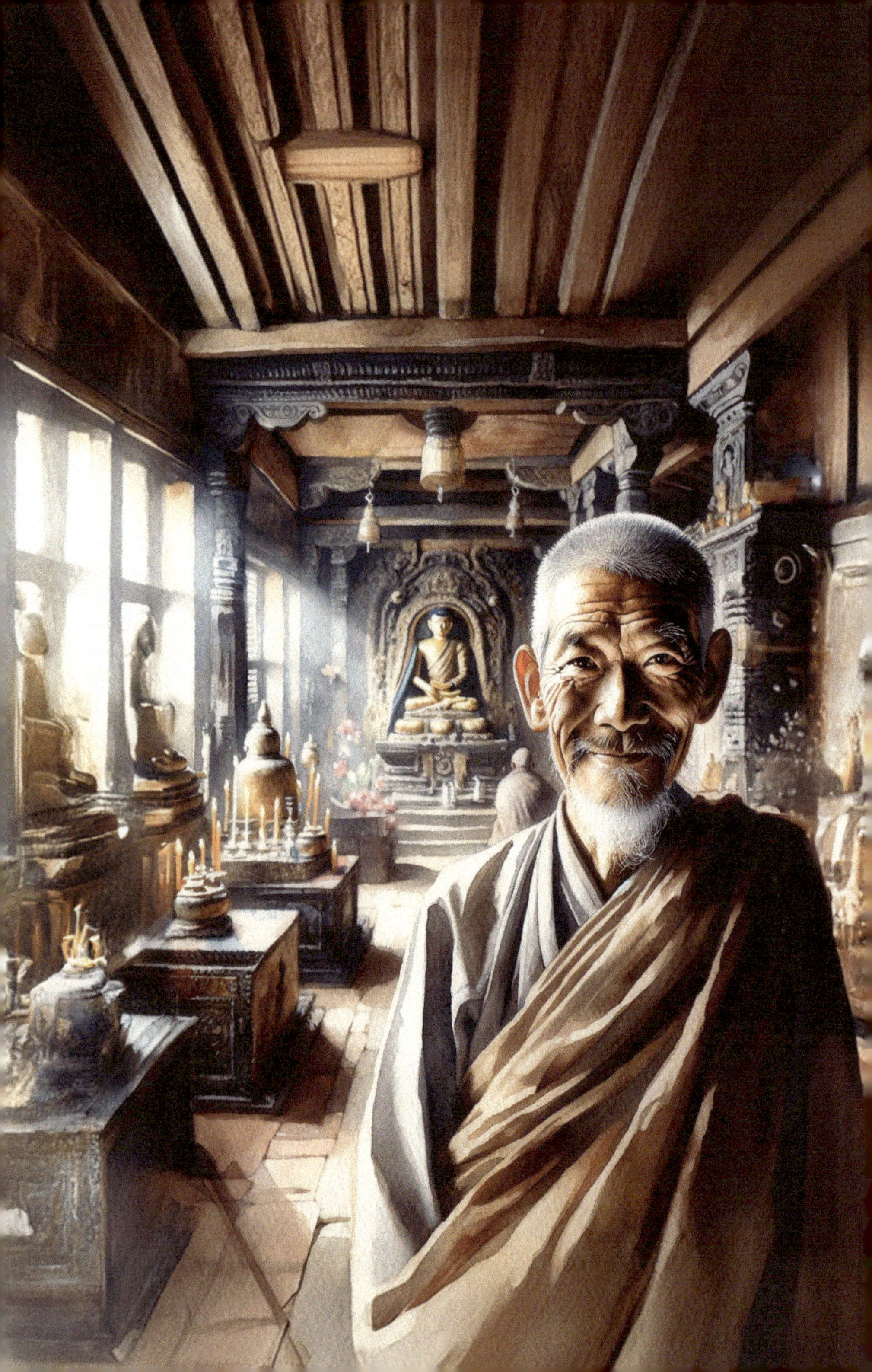

one of the most powerful tools for doing so is the practice of ritual."

Nat felt a flicker of curiosity at his words. She had always associated rituals with religious or cultural traditions, not with the world of mountaineering. "What kind of ritual?"

"The secret kind!" Sonam whispered, causing a ripple of laughter from Nat and Evie.

He spread his hands wide. "A ritual is simply a set of actions performed with intention and awareness. It can be as simple as taking a few deep breaths before starting a climb, or as complex as a series of movements and meditations designed to bring the mind and body into alignment. The key is to approach the ritual with a sense of purpose and presence, to allow it to become a doorway into a deeper state of focus and connection." He motioned to them. "Come, let me share with you a ritual that has served me well—a way of preparing the mind and body for the challenges ahead."

Nat and Evie followed Sonam's lead as he guided them through a series of slow, deliberate movements. They began with a simple standing meditation, with feet rooted to the ground, shoulders back, and eyes closed. Sonam encouraged them to focus on their breath, to let go of any distracting thoughts or worries and simply be present in the moment.

As they moved through the ritual, Nat grew more relaxed. The gentle stretches and flowing movements released tension she didn't realize she was holding, leaving her feeling centered and energized.

"The power of ritual," Sonam said as they finished the sequence, "lies in its ability to bring us into a state of heightened awareness and focus. When we engage in a ritual with intention and presence, we create a space where our minds are free from distraction, where we can tap into a deeper source of strength and resilience."

"I've experienced that myself," Evie said. "There have been times on climbs where I've felt scattered or overwhelmed, but by taking a moment to center myself through ritual, I've been able to find a sense of clarity and purpose that carries me through."

"Yes," Sonam said. "The mountain has a way of stripping away the nonessential, of forcing us to confront ourselves in a very direct and immediate way. And it is in those moments of challenge and uncertainty that the power of presence and focus becomes most apparent." He turned to Nat. "Think of a time in your own climbing when a lack of focus held you back. A moment when your mind was pulled in different directions, when doubt or fear clouded your judgment."

Nat paused, reflecting on her own experiences. She thought of a climb she had attempted the previous year, a demanding route that had pushed her to her limits. There had been a crux move—the hardest and most precarious of a delicate sequence of maneuvers that required absolute precision and commitment. But in the moment, she had hesitated, her mind suddenly flooded with thoughts of failure and consequence.

"I can think of a few," she admitted. "Times when I've gotten in my own way, when I've allowed my thoughts to spiral out of control instead of staying focused on the task at hand."

Sonam nodded. "It is a challenge we all face. The mind can be our greatest ally or our greatest obstacle. But through the practice of ritual, we can learn to harness its power, to direct our focus and attention in a way that serves us."

As they made their way toward base camp, the conversation flowed easily. The Sherpa's words had sparked a deep reflection in both climbers, and they were eager to explore the concepts further.

"Sonam," Nat said, adjusting her pack as they navigated a rocky stretch of trail. "What you said about the power of ritual to bring focus and presence... I've had moments on climbs where I've felt that sense of clarity, but I never quite understood how to access it consistently."

"It is a practice, like any other," Sonam said. "The more you cultivate it, the more readily it will come to you. But it is not just about the ritual itself. It's the intention behind it, the willingness to let go of distraction and fully embrace the present moment."

"Summoning that clarity at will is a lifelong challenge," Evie said. "I still struggle with it. Sometimes I've been so caught up in my own thoughts, my own worries and fears, that I've lost sight of what's right in front of me. But when I've been able to let go of that mental chatter and just be present, it's like everything comes into sharper focus. The climb, my movements, the surrounding environment—it all seems to flow more easily."

"Yes," Sonam said. "The mind can be a powerful tool, but it can also be a great hindrance. It is easy to get lost in the labyrinth of our own thoughts, to become disconnected from the reality of the moment. But when we learn to quiet the mind, to bring our full attention to the present, we open ourselves up to a deeper level of experience and understanding."

He paused for a moment, seeming to gather his thoughts. "I remember a climb I undertook many years ago. It was a challenging route, one that I had attempted before but never successfully completed. I had built it up in my mind as this great obstacle, this insurmountable barrier to my progress as a climber. On the day of the climb, I found myself consumed by doubt and fear. Every move felt uncertain, every hold tenuous. My mind was constantly racing ahead, anticipating all the ways things could go wrong. But then, at a critical moment, I remembered a simple ritual my father had taught me, a way of centering myself and focusing my energy."

He closed his eyes for a moment, as if reliving the memory. "I took a deep breath and began to recite a mantra, a short phrase that had always brought me a sense of calm and clarity. As I repeated the words, I felt my mind begin to settle, my focus narrowing to the task at hand. And with each movement, each breath, I felt a sense of flow and connection that I had never experienced before. It was as if the mountain and I were moving as one, in perfect harmony with the present moment."

Nat could relate to that feeling, rare as it was in her experience. "I've had moments like that. Where everything else falls away and there's just this sense of pure, unfiltered presence. It's a feeling of being fully alive, fully engaged with the world around you."

"Exactly," Sonam said. "And it is a feeling that we can cultivate—not just in our climbing, but in every aspect of our lives. By bringing a sense of ritual and intention to our actions, by making a practice of presence and focus, we open ourselves up to a deeper level of experience and connection, a way of being that is more fully awake and alive."

The following day, as they began their ascent of Mount Thamserku, Nat integrated elements of Sonam's ritual into her preparation. She took a moment before each push to center herself, to focus on her breath and set clear intentions for her movements. And to her surprise, she found that the practice

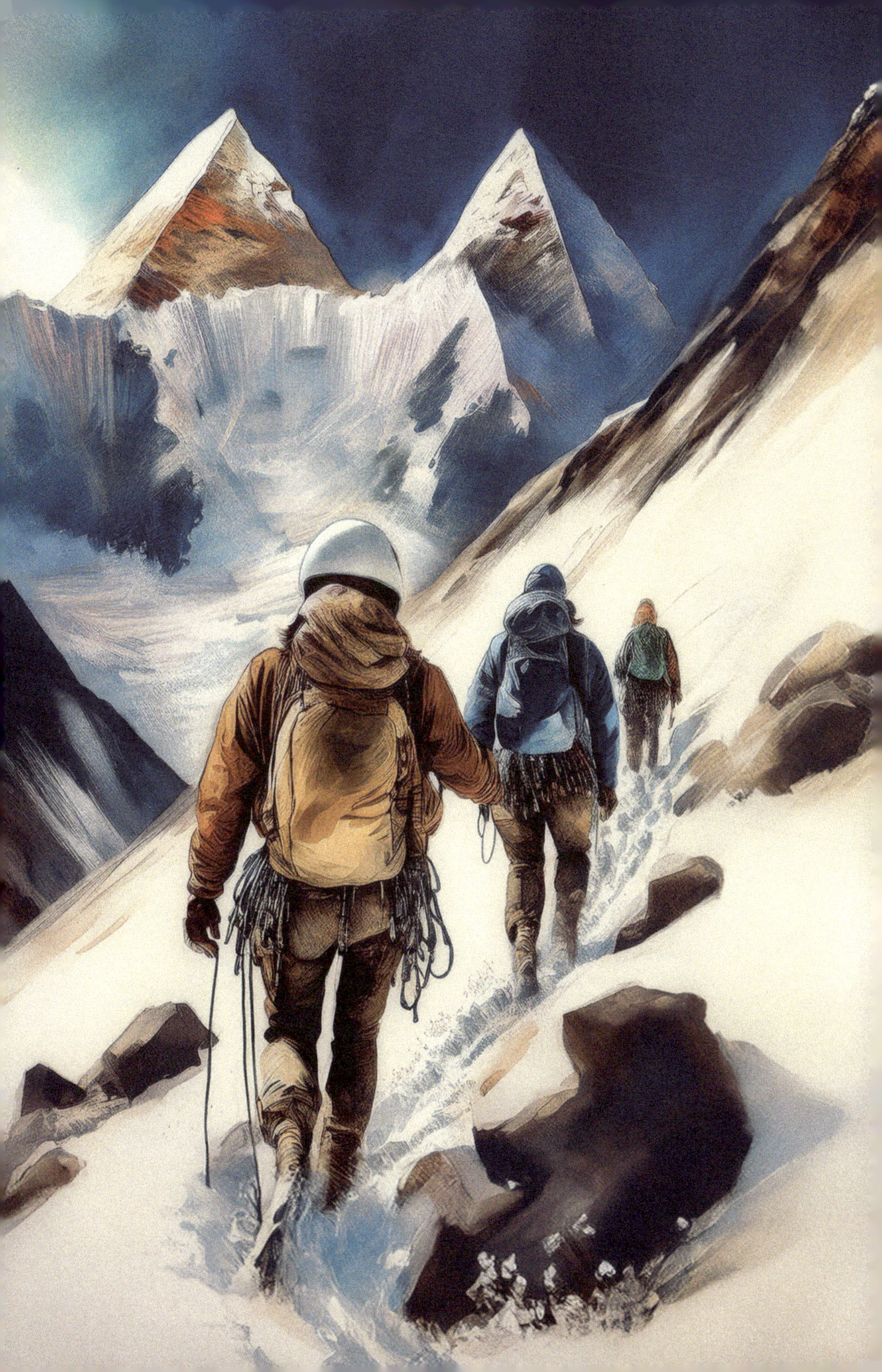

had an almost immediate effect. Her mind felt sharper, her movements more precise and purposeful. Even in the face of challenging conditions and unexpected setbacks, she was able to maintain a sense of presence and focus that allowed her to adapt and persevere.

"The mountain demands our full attention, our complete presence," Sonam said as they rested at a high camp, the vast expanse of the Himalayas stretching out before them. "And in return, it offers us a glimpse of something profound, a connection to a deeper truth that lies within us all."

Nat thought of all the climbs she had undertaken, all the challenges she had faced and overcome. She realized that in each of those moments, she had been tapping into a wellspring of strength and resilience that came from a place of deep presence and focus.

"You know," Evie said, "this reminds me of a major expedition I led years ago. It was a logistically complex project that required coordinating multiple teams, permits, and suppliers, and I often felt overwhelmed by the sheer scale of it all. But by starting each day with a simple ritual—taking a few moments to sit in silence, set my intentions, and visualize a successful outcome—I found I was able to approach the challenges with a greater sense of clarity, focus, and purpose."

"Rituals for the win!" Nat said.

Evie laughed. "Darn right!"

As they neared the summit of Mount Thamserku, Nat realized that like the other lessons, the practices Sonam had taught them were not just tools for climbing, but for life itself—a way of navigating ups and downs with grace and resilience. And when they finally stood atop the peak, the world falling away on all sides in a dizzying expanse of snow and sky, Nat felt a connection, a deep knowing that she was exactly where she was meant to be.

"Remember," Sonam said later as they prepared to descend. "The true summit is not the top of the mountain, but the stillness at the center of your being. Cultivate that stillness, that presence and focus, and you will find that there is nothing you cannot achieve—no challenge you cannot meet with an open heart and a clear mind."

"That mantra from your story," Nat said. "What was it?"

Sonam smiled. "With intention, I begin. With presence, I climb."

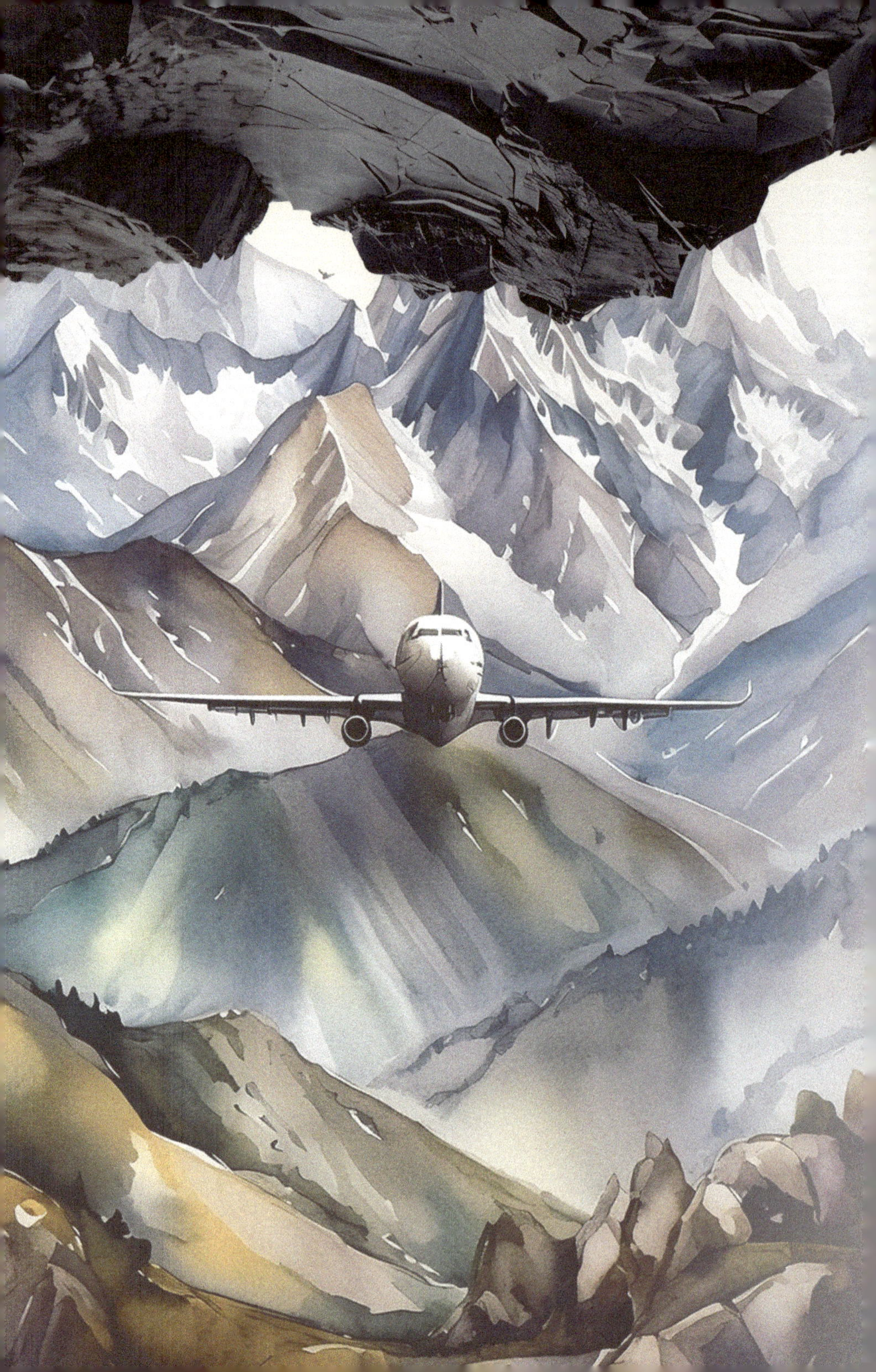

9 The Beginner's Mindset

• ● ● •

Nat gazed out the window of the small twin-engine plane as it soared over the rugged terrain of Pakistan. The jagged peaks, vast glaciers, and shadowed valleys were a stark contrast to the majestic snow-capped giants and deep, forested gorges of the Khumbu region they had left behind.

Beside her, Evie sat quietly, her eyes closed in meditation. The two women had been traveling for hours, making their way from Islamabad to Skardu, the gateway to the Karakoram mountain range, where their next challenge awaited them.

Nat's mind drifted back to the lessons she had learned, the insights she had gained. Each mountain, each Sherpa, had given her a piece of the puzzle, a glimpse into a way of being that was at once ancient and utterly new.

She thought of Tenzin's attunement to the present moment, Lhakpa's unwavering faith, Dawa's joyful embrace of challenges, and Sonam's ritual practice. They had shown her that the true summit, the real journey, was not in the conquering of peaks, but in the exploration of the soul.

She turned to Evie, curiosity getting the better of her. "So, where exactly are we headed next? You've been pretty tight-lipped about our destination."

Evie opened her eyes, a mischievous grin playing at the corners of her mouth. "Oh, you know, just a little place called the Ogre."

Nat's eyebrows shot up. "Baintha Brakk? This should be fun."

"One of the most beautiful and challenging peaks of the Karakoram."

"Beautiful and challenging," Nat mused. "Seems to be a theme with the mountains you choose."

Evie's grin widened. "What can I say? I like to keep things interesting. And remember, if you need me to carry any of your gear up the mountain for you, just let me know."

Nat barked a laugh. "Yeah, take my pack. That way, I can carry you up on piggy-back."

Evie snickered as her eyes drifted closed.

Chuckling, Nat turned her gaze back to the window. Whatever challenges lay ahead, she was glad she had Evie by her side.

The jeep bumped and rattled along the narrow, winding track, kicking up clouds of dust in its wake. Nat braced herself against the doorframe, her body jostled by the uneven terrain as she peered out at the stark, unforgiving landscape of the Karakoram.

Beside her, Evie seemed utterly unperturbed by the rough ride. "I wanted to save the best for last," she shouted over the roar of the engine. "It doesn't get much better than Baintha Brakk."

Nat had heard stories about the mountain called the Ogre—whispers of its sheer technical difficulty and punishing conditions. It was a peak that had repelled all but the most skilled and determined of climbers, a test piece that pushed even the elites to their absolute limits. "You sure I'm ready for this?" she asked, only half-joking. "I mean, I know we've had some epic climbs so far, but from what I've heard, Baintha Brakk is on a whole different level."

Evie's grin only widened. "Oh, you're ready, alright. More ready than you know. But the real question is, are you willing?"

Before Nat could ask what she meant, the jeep lurched to a stop at the base of a massive, looming wall of rock and ice. Nat felt her breath catch in her throat as she craned her neck to take in the full scale of the challenge before her, the sheer audacity of the mountain's defenses.

As they clambered out of the vehicle, stretching limbs stiff from the long journey, a figure emerged from a nearby tent.

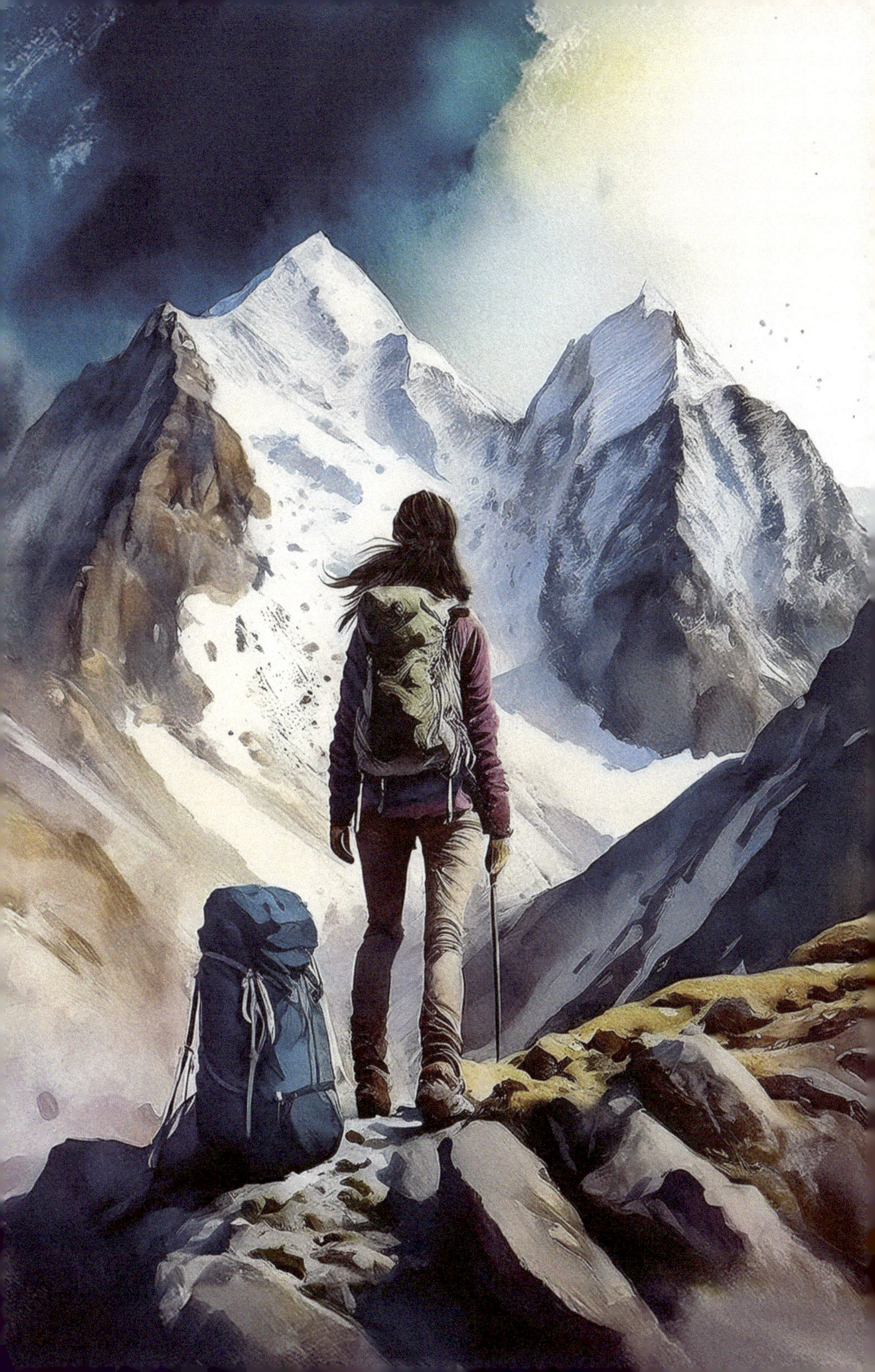

Nat blinked, taking in the woman's shock of white hair, the weathered, angular features, the piercing blue eyes that seemed to see straight through her.

"Pasang," Evie said, striding forward to clasp the Sherpa's hand. "It's good to see you, my friend. I've brought someone special to meet you."

Pasang's gaze shifted to her, and Nat felt herself straighten under the weight of the appraisal. There was something in the set of Pasang's jaw, the quiet intensity of her bearing, that spoke of a lifetime spent in the unforgiving crucible of the high mountains.

"Natalia Rivera," Pasang said, her voice low yet melodious. "You've achieved much, for one so young."

Nat inclined her head. "Thank you, Pasang. That means a great deal, coming from you."

Pasang only gave her a noncommittal nod before gesturing toward the distant mountain with a sweep of her arm. "Baintha Brakk cares nothing for your achievements or reputation. Here, on this mountain, you are a novice. If you wish to stand upon its summit, you must let go of all you think you know."

Nat felt a flicker of defiance, a reflexive urge to defend her hard-won expertise. But something in Pasang's tone, in the unflinching directness of her gaze, made her pause. There was a challenge there, yes, but also an invitation. A call to step outside the confines of her own certitude, to embrace the unknown.

As they began their preparations for the climb, sorting gear and studying maps, Pasang continued to press Nat, to probe at the edges of her comfort zone. She questioned Nat's choice of route, her selection of equipment, the very fundamentals of her approach.

At first, Nat bristled under the constant scrutiny, the relentless pressure to justify her every decision. But as the hours wore on, as she found herself engaged in a deep and probing dialogue with the enigmatic Sherpa, something began to shift within her.

She thought of all the climbs she had undertaken, all the peaks she had conquered. And she realized, with a start, how much of her success had been built upon a foundation of familiarity, of tried-and-true methods and techniques. She had become an expert, yes, but at what cost? How much had she closed herself off to new ideas, new possibilities, in the pursuit of mastery?

Evie, watching the exchange with a knowing glint in her eye, chimed in with a story. "You know, when I first started climbing with Pasang, I thought I had it all figured out. I had dozens of expeditions under my belt. I didn't think there was much a Sherpa could teach me that I didn't already know. But Pasang, she has a way of cutting through all the noise, of stripping away the layers of ego and assumption. She forced me to confront my own limitations and blind spots. In doing so, she opened up a whole new world of possibility."

Pasang nodded, her eyes distant. "The mountain is a great equalizer. It cares nothing for your titles or trophies. It demands only that you come to it with an open heart and a willing spirit. If you can let go of your preconceptions and embrace the lessons it has to offer, then and only then will you find the true summit."

As they set out on the first stage of the climb, picking their way up the mountain's lower flanks, Nat felt the weight of Pasang's words settling over her. She had come to Baintha Brakk expecting a challenge, yes, but one that would test her physical strength and technical skill. She hadn't expected this

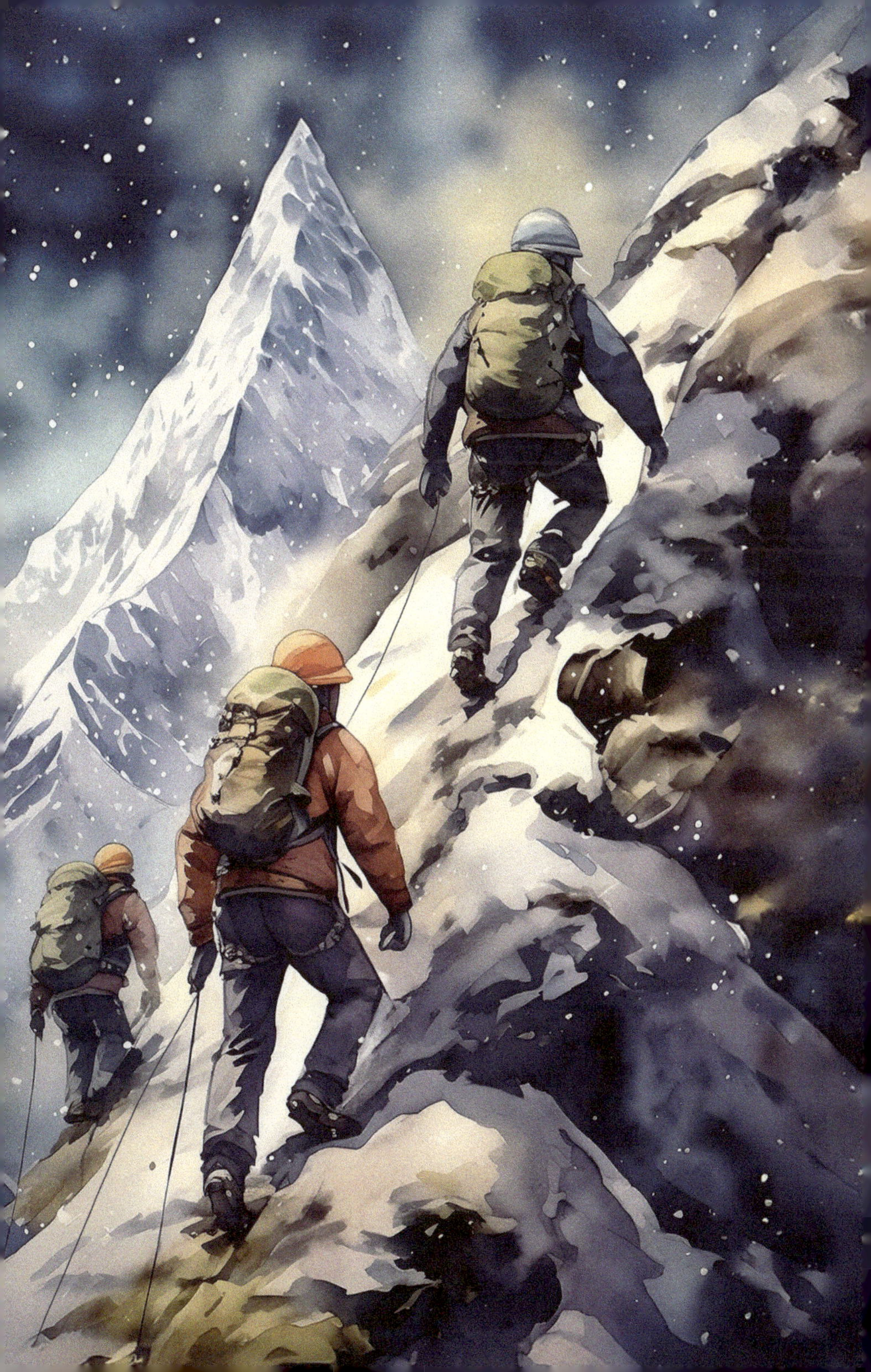

other trial, this confrontation with her own psyche—her own deeply ingrained patterns of thought and behavior.

The higher they climbed, the more punishing the conditions became. The thin air seared Nat's lungs, the cold bit through even her most insulated layers. The technical difficulties of the route seemed to compound with every vertical meter gained.

And through it all, Pasang pushed her relentlessly. The old Sherpa set a blistering pace, forcing Nat to dig deep into her reserves of strength and stamina. Pasang chose the most challenging lines, the most exposed and committing sequences, as if daring Nat to balk and retreat into the safety of the known. There were moments, high on those storm-lashed faces, when Nat felt her confidence waver, her belief in her own abilities flicker and dim. The old doubts and insecurities came creeping back in, whispering that she wasn't strong enough or skilled enough to meet this test.

But always, just when she felt herself on the verge of succumbing, Pasang's voice would cut through the clamor of her thoughts, stern yet strangely comforting. "Breathe, Natalia," she would say, her tone brooking no argument. "Focus on the present, the task at hand. Let go of what you think you know, and trust in the learning that comes with each moment."

And so Nat breathed. She focused. She let go, again and again, of the expectations and assumptions that had held her back, that had kept her tethered to a narrow view of her own potential. And slowly, inch by inch, she began to find a new way forward, a new path up the mountain.

There was a moment, high on the final headwall, where the magnitude of the challenge before her seemed to crystalize into a single, impossible obstacle—a blank stretch of overhanging granite, devoid of any obvious holds or features.

Nat felt her heart sink, her breath coming in shallow gasps as she contemplated the sheer improbability of it. She had faced tough sections before, had pushed through cruxes that seemed beyond her abilities at first. But this... this felt different, a challenge of an entirely different order.

Beside her, Evie and Pasang exchanged a glance. Evie turned to Nat, her expression a mix of sympathy and encouragement. "I know that feeling," she said, her voice barely audible over the keening of the wind. "That moment when the mountain seems to ask more of you than you have to give, when every instinct is screaming at you to back down, to give up." She reached out, laying a gloved hand on Nat's shoulder. "But this is where the real learning happens, Nat. This is where you find out what you're truly made of. Not as a climber, but as a human being."

Pasang nodded, her eyes shining with an almost feral intensity. "The mountain is a mirror, Natalia. It reflects our own limitations, fears, and doubts. But it also shows us our strength, if we are willing to look." She gestured toward the implacable granite of the headwall. "This section, it is not here to defeat you, but to teach you. To force you to let go of your ego, your assumptions, and approach the problem with a beginner's mind and a learner's heart."

Nat felt a shiver run through her. How many times had she faced a similar choice—to retreat into the familiar or step forward into the unknown?

She thought of all the climbs that had come before, all the lessons learned and the wisdom gained. And she knew with a sudden, unshakeable certainty that the mountain was offering her the greatest lesson of all.

With a deep breath, she unclipped from the anchor, feeling the weight of the rope settle onto her harness. She looked up at the headwall, at the impossible blankness of the stone. And then she began to climb, one move at a time, her mind emptied of all expectation, all anticipation.

Her body found holds and sequences her conscious mind could never have conceived of. There was no past, no future, only the eternal present of each placement, each breath, each micro-adjustment of balance and positioning. And through it all, Pasang's voice drifted up to her, an anchor in the maelstrom of sensation and exertion. "Yes, Natalia. Let go, let flow. The mountain will show you the way, if you let it."

And so Nat let go, time and again, of all that she had been, all that she had known. She let the mountain strip her down to her essential self, to the core of her being that was pure presence, pure potential. In that letting go, that radical surrender, she found a freedom and a joy she had never known before—a lightness of being that was as vast as the sky itself.

As they stood together on the summit of Baintha Brakk, the world falling away on all sides in a dizzying sprawl of rock and ice and sky, Nat felt a centeredness as solid and unshakeable as the mountain itself. She had found a new way of approaching challenge and opportunity. A new way of climbing. A new way of being.

She had learned on the savage flanks of the Ogre that true mastery was not about reaching the summit, but about embracing the climb itself. About approaching each moment, each obstacle, with a beginner's mind and an open heart, willing to be humbled and transformed by the lessons that the mountain—and life itself—had to offer. With that knowledge, that wisdom, she knew she was ready for whatever peaks, valleys, and uncharted territories awaited her.

She understood that the greatest adventure of all was the one that led ever inward—ever deeper into the vast and untapped potential of her own being.

The Beginner's Mindset

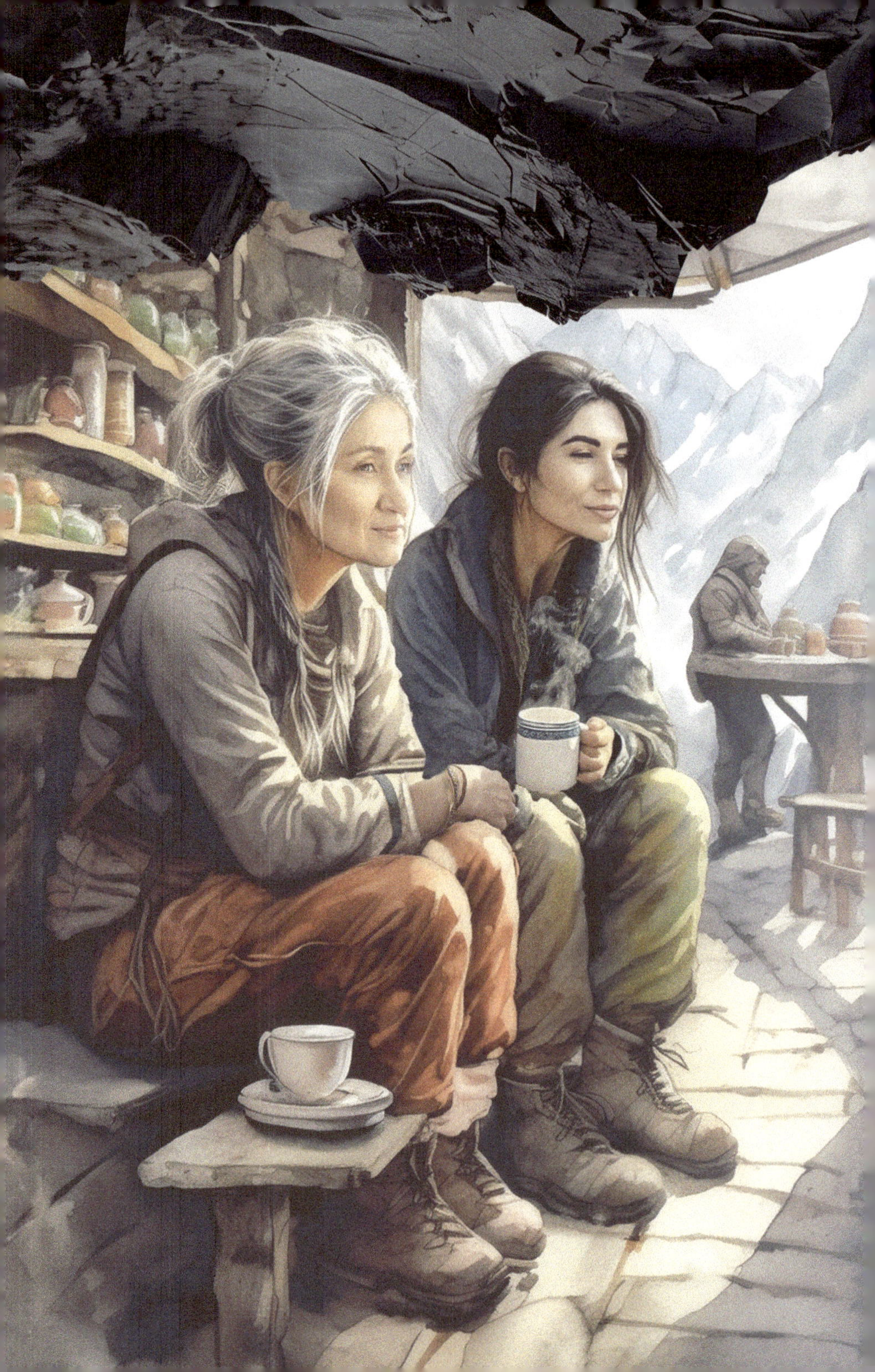

10 A Changed Woman

The descent from the summit of Baintha Brakk was a blur of exhaustion and elation, a dreamlike journey through a landscape transformed by the lens of experience. As Nat picked her way down the mountain's flanks, her body moving with a fluid grace born of confidence, she felt as though she were inhabiting a new skin.

Beside her, Evie moved with a similar ease, her face radiating a quiet joy that spoke of deep contentment, of hard-fought battles won and lessons learned. They exchanged few words as they navigated the complex terrain, but the silence between them was rich with understanding—an unspoken bond of shared struggle and triumph.

It was only when they reached base camp, their bodies aching with fatigue but their spirits soaring, that the full weight of the journey began to settle over Nat. As she sat on a bench next to Evie, cradling a mug of steaming tea in her hands, she felt a wave of emotion rise up within her, a complex tangle of gratitude and awe and humility.

"I feel like I've been given a gift," she said, her gaze fixed on the distant silhouette of the mountain. "Like each of the Sherpas, in their own way, has handed me a key to a door I didn't even know existed."

"That's the power of these teachings," Evie said. "They have a way of sneaking up on you—changing you in ways you never could have anticipated." She leaned back, her face tilted toward the vast expanse of the sky. "I remember my first time climbing with Tenzin, on the Matterhorn. He was so patient, so attuned to the subtle rhythms of the mountain. He taught me to find beauty in the smallest moments, to see the sacred in the mundane."

Nat nodded, a memory surfacing. "Tenzin said something on that climb. He said, 'Success leaves clues.' At the time, I didn't fully understand what he meant. But now I think I'm starting to see." She paused, searching for the words. "It's like every challenge, every setback, every moment of doubt, they're all part of the journey, all clues to something greater. And if we can learn to read those clues, to see the lessons in the struggle… then we open ourselves up to a whole new understanding of what it means to be alive."

"Yes," Evie said. "That's it exactly."

They sat in silence for a long moment, each lost in their own reflections. Then Evie spoke again, her voice soft with wonder.

"You know, when I first started this journey with you, I thought I was the one who would be doing the teaching. I thought I had all the answers, all the wisdom to impart. But watching you grow, seeing you confront your own fears and limitations with such courage and grace—it's been a revelation." A laugh bubbled up from deep within. "The student becomes the teacher, and the teacher becomes the student. Isn't that always the way?"

Nat grinned, feeling a surge of affection for her friend and mentor. "We're all learning from each other. That's the beauty of it, the gift of it. No one has all the answers, but together, we can find our way forward, one step at a time."

They sipped their tea as the sun began its slow descent toward the horizon. Nat let her mind wander, revisiting the moments and memories that had shaped her over the past weeks and months.

She thought of Lhakpa, the fierce and uncompromising guide who had pushed her to the limits of her endurance on the sheer faces of the Trango Tower. *Fear and faith cannot coexist,* Lhakpa had told her, his eyes boring into hers with an intensity that had left her breathless. *You must choose one or the other, and live with the consequences of that choice.*

At the time, Nat had struggled with the starkness of that pronouncement, had railed against the idea that she had to somehow banish fear in order to find true strength. But now, looking back, she saw the wisdom in his words, the invitation to lean into the discomfort, to trust in something greater than herself.

"Lhakpa taught me that courage isn't the absence of fear," she said, giving voice to the realization as it crystallized within her. "It's the willingness to face that fear, to move through it and beyond it. To choose faith, even when every instinct is screaming at you to run and hide."

Evie nodded, her expression thoughtful. "And Dawa, on Ama Dablam? What did she show you, in that high and holy place?"

Nat smiled, remembering the irrepressible Nepali woman, her infectious laughter and deceptively simple wisdom. "Dawa taught me to question my own assumptions and limiting beliefs. She showed me that the stories we tell ourselves, the narratives we cling to... they're just that—stories. We have the power to rewrite them, to create a new reality with every choice we make." She marveled at the profundity of that insight. "For so long, I'd been telling myself that I wasn't enough, that my worth was tied to my achievements. But Dawa, she saw right through that, to the truth of who I was beneath all the layers of fear and self-doubt. And she challenged me to see it too, to believe in my own inherent value and boundless potential."

Evie's eyes shined with pride. "And you rose to that challenge, Nat. You did the hard work of confronting those beliefs, digging deep and uprooting them at the source. That takes a special bravery—a willingness to be vulnerable and honest with yourself."

Nat felt a flush of warmth at the praise, a sense of quiet satisfaction at how far she had come. "I couldn't have done it without you all. Tenzin, Lhakpa, Dawa, Mingma, Sonam, Pasang… each of them gave me a piece of the puzzle, a glimpse of a greater truth. But you, Evie. You were the one who brought it all together." She reached out, clasping Evie's hand in her own. "Your wisdom, your guidance, your belief in me. They're a light in the darkness. I can't begin to express how grateful I am, how much your friendship means to me."

Evie squeezed Nat's hand, her eyes glistening with unshed tears. "Oh, the feeling is entirely mutual. Watching you grow, seeing you come into your own, it's been one of the greatest

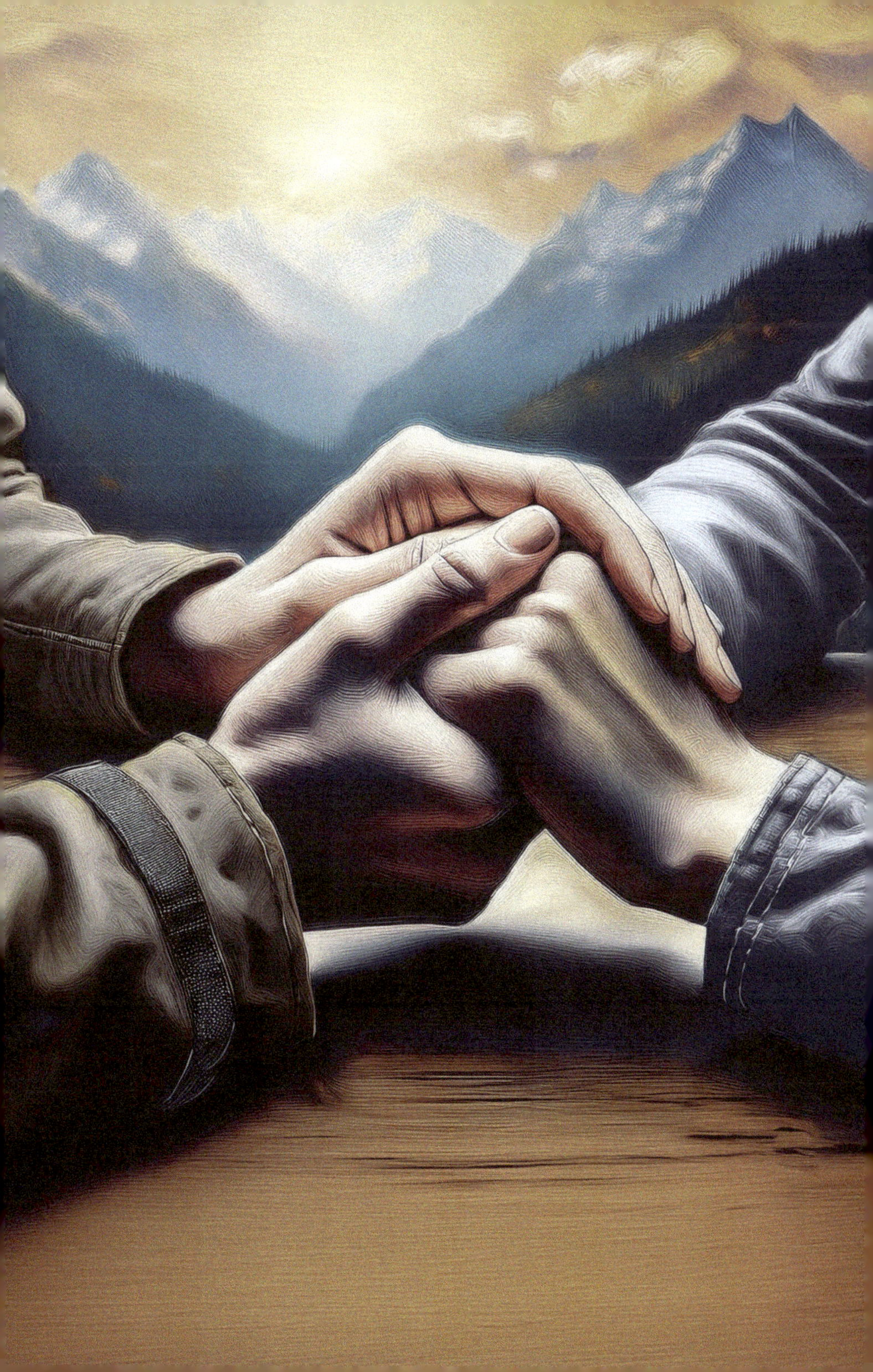

joys of my life." She paused, her gaze distant. "You know, even after all these years, all these climbs, the lessons of the Sherpas continue to guide me, to shape the way I move through the world. Tenzin's attunement to the present moment, Lhakpa's fierce and uncompromising faith, Dawa's joyful questioning of the status quo. They're all a part of me now, woven into the fabric of my being."

"I think that's the power of these teachings," Nat said, giving voice to the realization as it formed within her. "They're not just platitudes or abstract concepts. They're lived experiences, visceral and immediate. And when we open ourselves up to them, when we let them sink into our bones, they change us. Fundamentally and irrevocably."

"And that's why we keep coming back," Evie said. "Why we keep seeking out these mountains, these teachers, these challenges. Because we know the journey is never really finished. There's always more to learn and more to become. Our greatness doesn't have external limitations, only internal ones."

Nat felt a shiver of excitement at the prospect—a sense of vast and uncharted territory stretching out before her. "And we don't have to do it alone. That's the beauty of it. We have each other, and the wider community of seekers and adventurers. We can learn from each other, support each other, challenge each other to be our best selves."

"Exactly," Evie murmured. "And like Pasang said, the mountain is a mirror, reflecting back to us our own strengths and weaknesses, our own fears and desires. But it's also a teacher, a guide, a friend. And if we approach it with humility and openness, with a willingness to be changed by the encounter, then there's no limit to what we can discover. No end to the journey of transformation."

Evie paused, breathing in a deep sigh. "Success is a tricky thing, Nat. It's what we all strive for, but it can also become a trap. There are so many ways that it can trip us up. Take motivation, for example. When you've already achieved your biggest goals, it can be tough to find new challenges that really inspire you. Then there's the fear of failure. When you're at the top of your game, the pressure to maintain that level of success can be overwhelming. It's easy to start playing it safe, avoiding risks that might threaten your reputation.

SURVIVING GREATNESS

"And let's not forget the isolation that comes with being at the top. When you're the best in your field, it can be lonely. There are fewer people who truly understand what you're going through, and it's easy to feel disconnected from your peers. And perhaps most dangerous, there's the question of identity. When your sense of self is so tied up in your accomplishments, it can be tough to separate who you are from what you've achieved.

"The elite achievers of the world, those few at the very apex of their field, all contend with some combination of these challenges. Even fewer come to recognize the ultimate truth of success."

Nat gazed up at the sky. "Achieving greatness is just the first step. Then you must learn to survive it."

Evie nodded, a look of pride in her eyes. "And how do you survive it?"

"By taking the lessons you learned along the way and turning them inward. Then you can redefine what greatness means to you."

"And what does greatness mean to you?"

Nat met her gaze and smiled. "Whatever I want it to mean. There's no limit to what it can mean as I grow stronger internally."

A Changed Woman

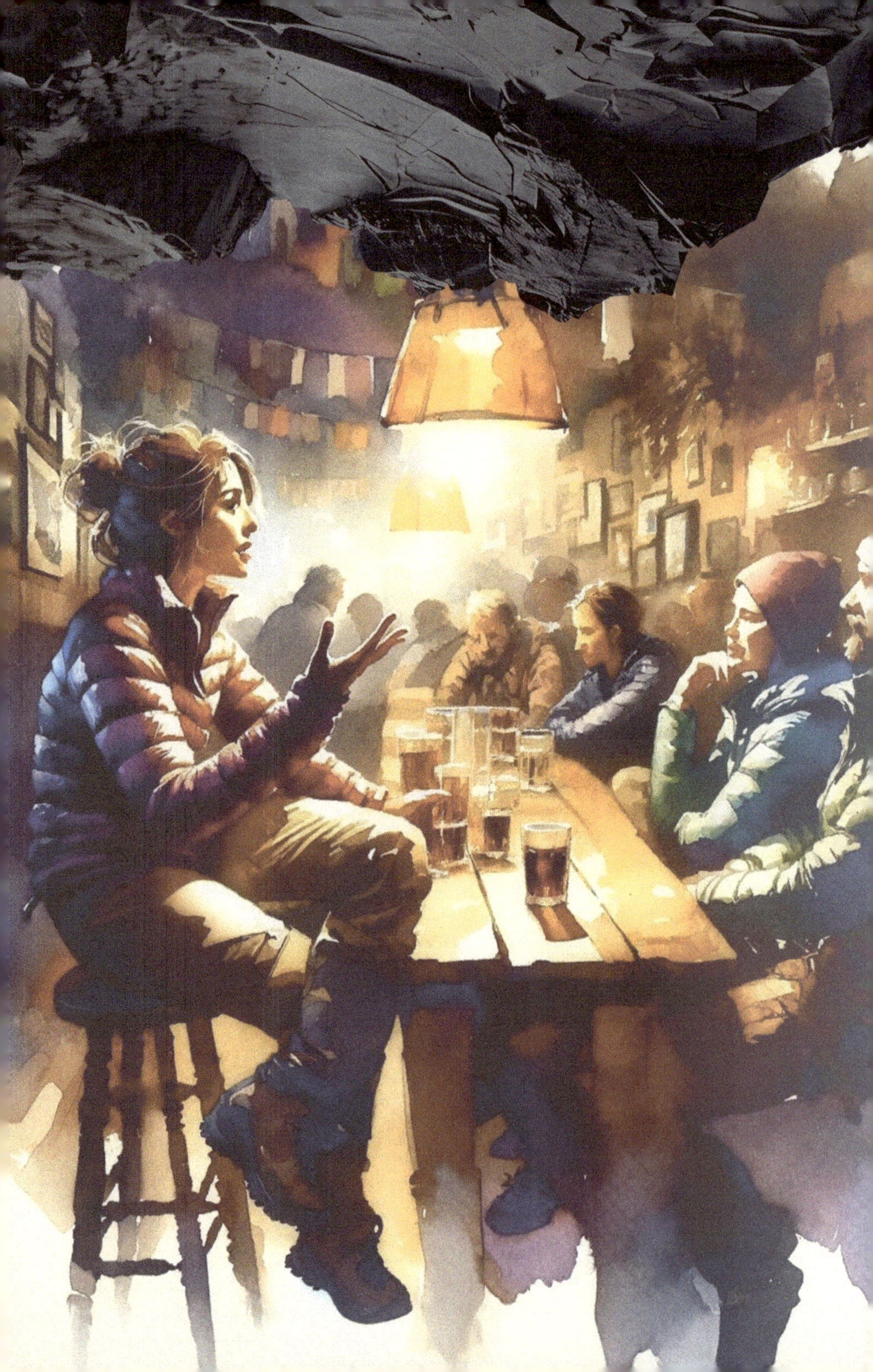

11

The Wild Places

• ● ● ● •

The return to everyday life was a gradual process for Nat—a gentle reintegration into the rhythms and routines of the familiar. She savored the small moments, the quiet rituals that had once seemed so mundane. The first sip of coffee in the morning, the feeling of sun on her skin as she walked to the climbing gym, the laughter of friends gathered around a campfire… each one felt imbued with new significance, giving her a deeper appreciation for the simple joy of being alive.

Yet it was in her climbing that Nat felt the most profound shift, a fundamental reorientation of her relationship to the sport that had defined her for so long. Where once she had approached each climb as a test to be passed, a summit to be conquered, now she found herself more interested in the journey itself, in the lessons and insights that each route had to offer.

She began to seek out climbs that challenged her not just physically, but mentally and emotionally. Routes that pushed her outside her comfort zone, that forced her to confront her own fears and limitations. And with each ascent, each moment of struggle and triumph, she felt herself growing, evolving, becoming more fully herself.

She also discovered a newfound appreciation for speaking—for passing on her experiences and the lessons she had learned. One evening, as she gave the keynote speech at a prominent annual mountaineering summit, Nat shared the story of her journey with Evie and the Sherpas to a rapt audience of hundreds. The room was silent, save for the occasional murmur or the rustle of someone shifting in their seat. All eyes were

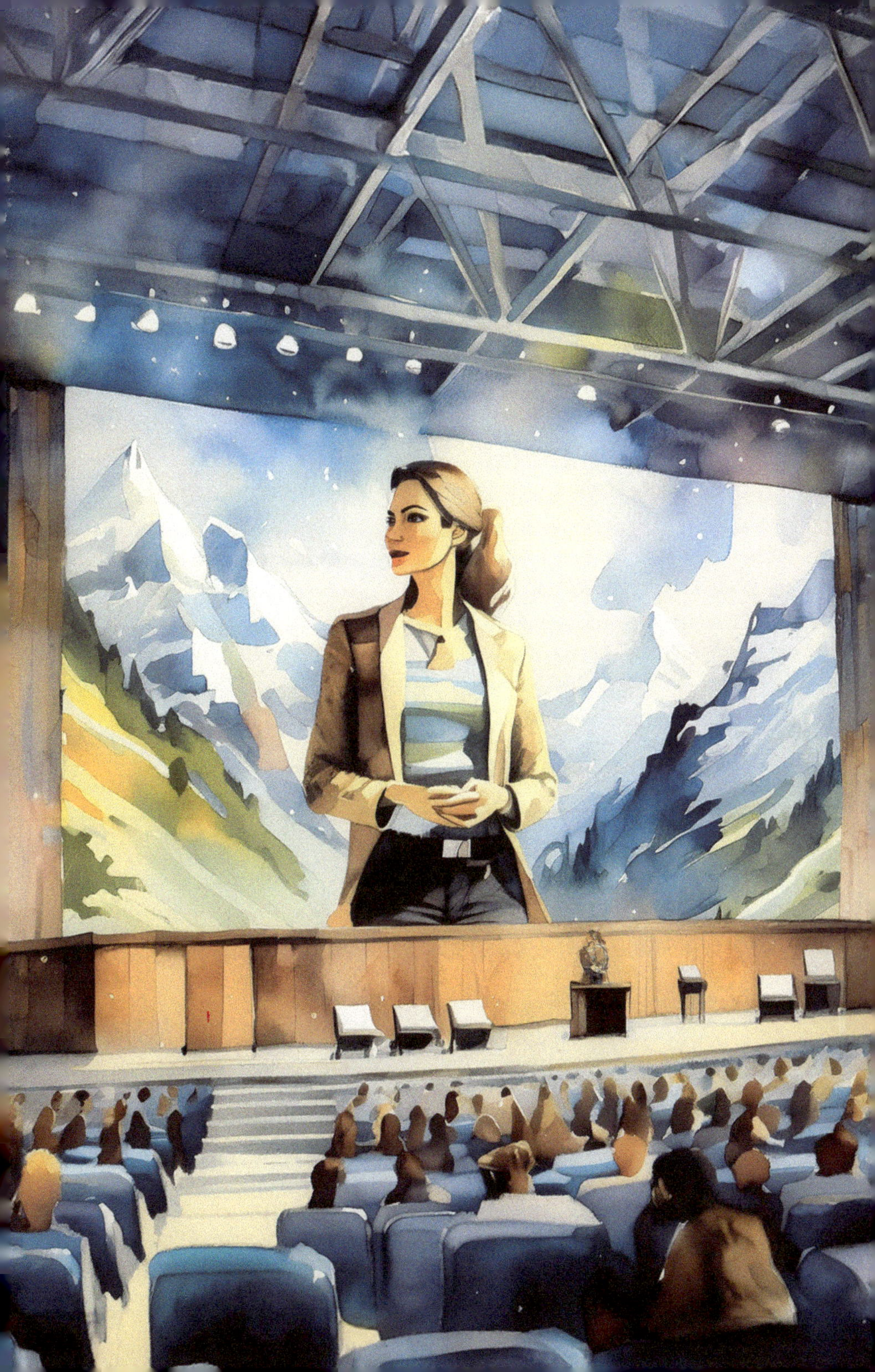

fixed on her, hanging on her every word as she wove a tale of self-discovery and transformation.

She spoke of the challenges she had faced, the lessons she had learned, the profound shift she had undergone. Her voice was clear and strong, resonating with the hard-won wisdom of someone who had been to the edge and back, who had wrestled with success and emerged victorious.

As she spoke, she saw the flicker of recognition in their eyes, the nods of understanding. And she realized her story was not unique—each of them had their own journey to undertake, their own path to walk, their own success to overcome.

"The mountain is a mirror, reflecting back to us our own strengths and weaknesses, our own potential for growth," Nat continued. "And if we can learn to approach each climb as an opportunity to learn and evolve, to push past our own limitations and fears, then we remember why we fell in love with climbing in the first place.

"We remember that climbing isn't about the summit—not really. It's about who we become in the process of reaching for it. It's about the lessons we learn, the bonds we forge, the moments of pure presence we experience along the way. The true gift of the mountains is the people they inspire us to become. They inspire us to stay true to ourselves, to make choices that align with our deepest values and aspirations, to embrace our vulnerability and lean into uncertainty.

"Yet none of us can do this alone. We need each other. Wisdom, love, and courage are at their most abundant in the company of kindred spirits. That's why we're all here today. That's the true summit. Not the peaks of the mountains, but the bonds we forge in our pursuit of those peaks.

"This is the gift of the wild places, the promise of the peaks. It's a journey that never ends—a horizon that beckons us ever onward, ever upward, to the very apex of our being."

She gave the crowd a smile. "The mountains are calling. I'll see you at the summit."

⛰️👟🎒

A few hours later, Nat sat alone in the bustling food court, the keynote crowd's cheers and applause still echoing in her mind. Lost in thought, it took her a moment to notice the young woman hovering nearby.

Nat recognized her immediately—Sasha Ivanov, a rising star in the climbing world. She was in her early twenties, with shoulder-length auburn hair and piercing green eyes. The woman's face was all over the internet and on every climbing magazine cover. Most recently, a series of impressive ascents in the Alps and the Andes had her name on everyone's lips. Yet Nat could sense that something was troubling her. There was an uncertainty to her bearing, a slight furrow in her brow that suggested an inner turmoil.

"Sasha, right?" Nat said, giving her a welcoming smile. "Please, grab a seat. I was hoping you'd attend the summit. I've been wanting to meet you."

"Thanks," Sasha said, sitting down. "It's really great to meet you. I've had your poster on my wall for years."

"Oh, that's very kind," Nat said. "You'll have to sign one of yours so I can add it to my own wall." She pushed her paper tray of fries into the middle of the table. "But first, why don't you help me with these fries and tell me what's bothering you?"

Sasha took a fry and dipped it in a small pool of ketchup, seeming to gather her thoughts. "Thanks. Uh, I don't really know where to begin, but your speech was kind of a punch in the gut for me. Like, everything I've been feeling lately..." She paused and let out a sigh. "More like the past year or two, actually. It's like you summed up everything I haven't been able to put into words."

Nat leaned forward. "Tell me more."

Over the next hour, Sasha poured her heart out. She spoke of the pressures she felt as a rising star in the climbing world, the constant need to push herself harder, to achieve more, to live up to the expectations of her sponsors and her fans. She confessed her doubts about her next big climb, a daunting peak in the Karakoram that had never been summited before.

"It's become all about the accolades, the sponsorships, the media attention," Sasha concluded. "All the things I thought I wanted, I finally have. And I've never felt more lost."

"I know the feeling," Nat said. "And I know just how to help you."

Sasha's eyebrows shot up. "You do?"

"Mm-hm. Here's the thing, Sasha. You've reached the top, and what you're wondering now is how to climb higher. But the fact is, there is no higher to climb. Nevertheless, your journey is just beginning."

"But if I can't go higher, where else is there to go?"

"Inward," Nat said. She let the word sink in as she studied the young woman. "How'd you like to join me on a trip?"

"Really?" Sasha said, her eyes wide. "I'd love to. Where?"

"Oh, here and there," Nat said with a smile. "There are a few people I'd like you to meet."

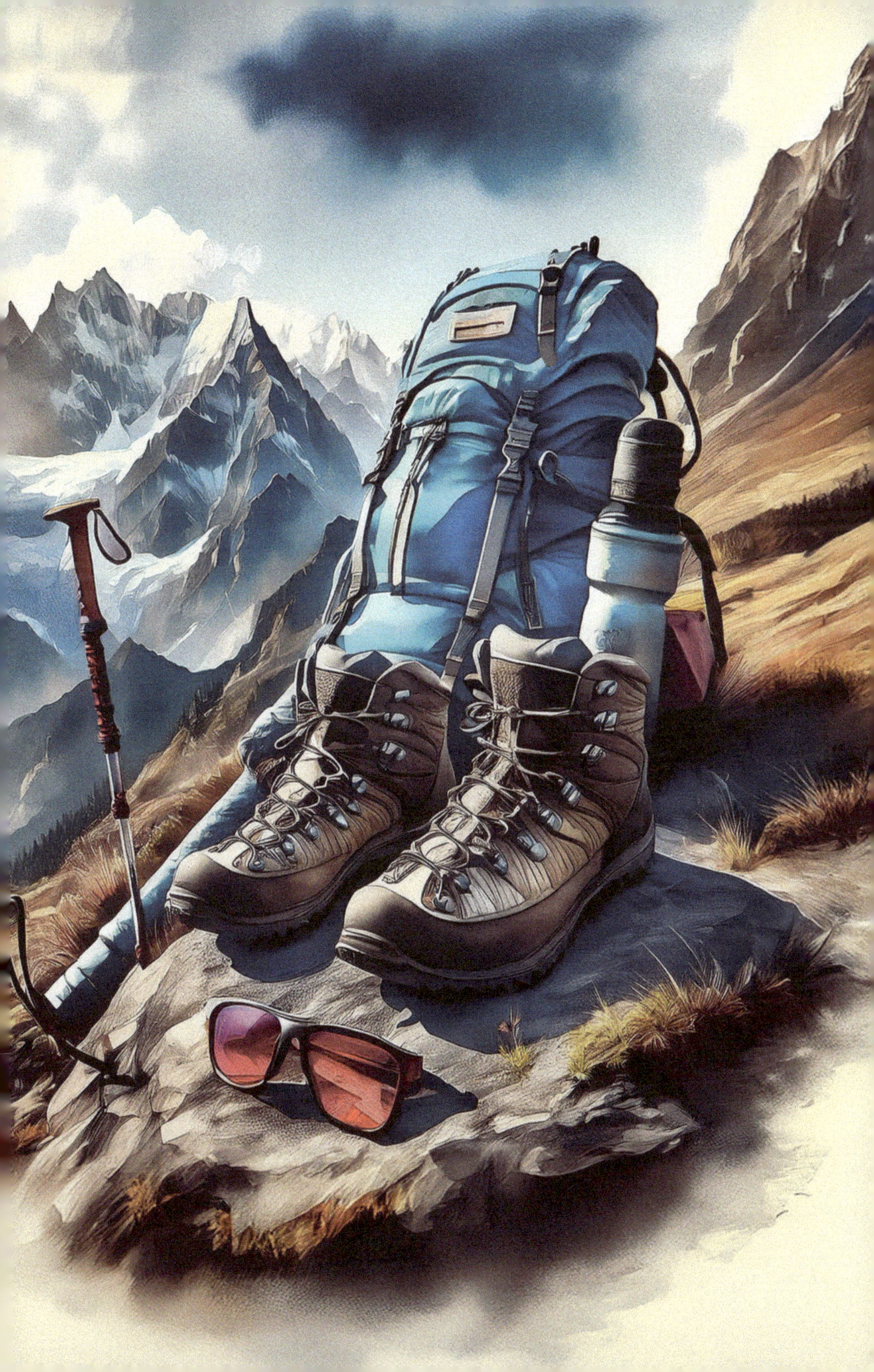

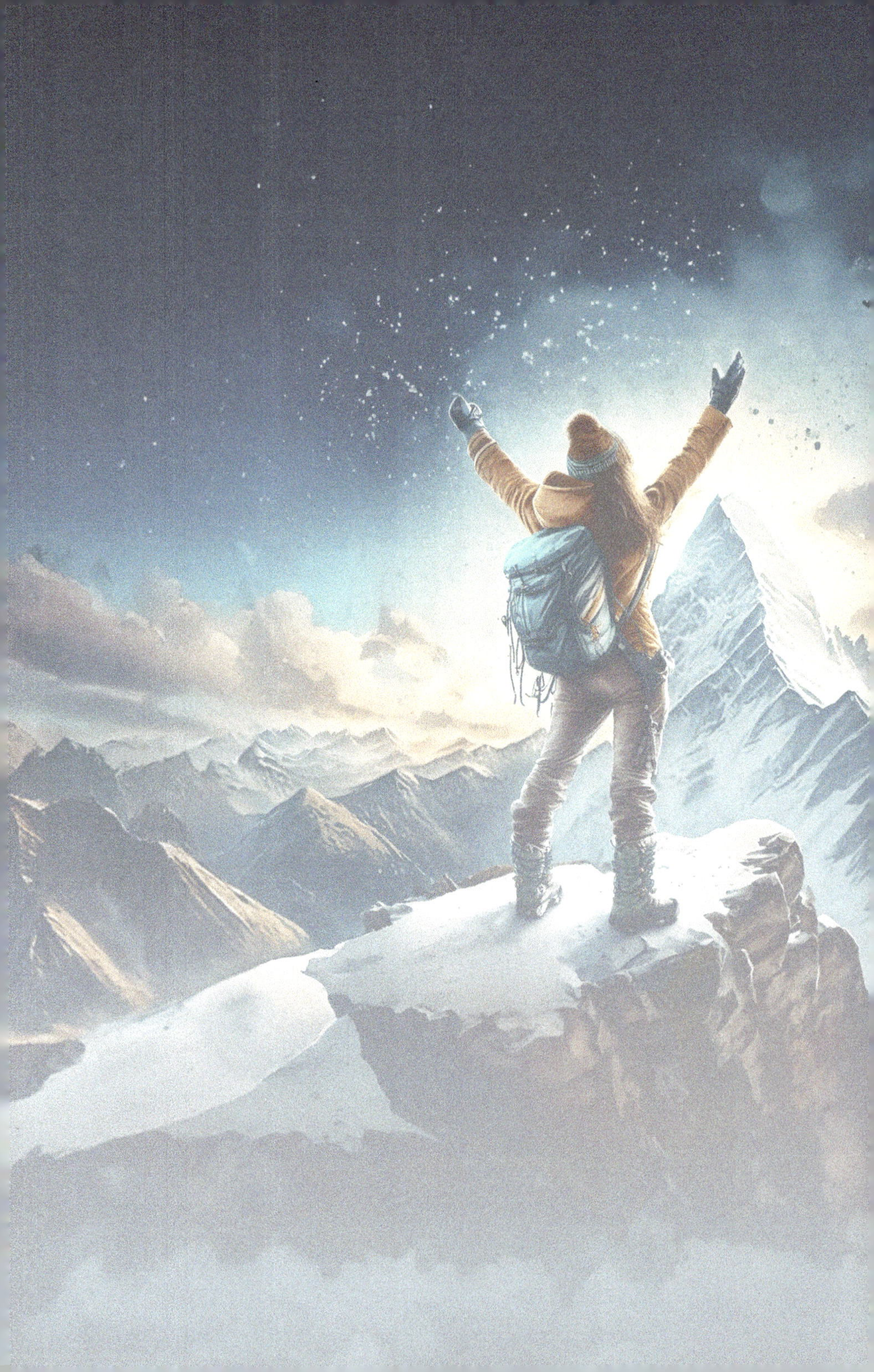

"SURVIVE YOUR GREATNESS

Milton Keynes UK
Ingram Content Group UK Ltd.
UKHW051350221124
451301UK00004BA/29